ELECTED TO DIE

Phil Gandon

PublishAmerica
Baltimore

PublishAmerica has allowed this work to remain exactly as the author intended, verbatim, without editorial input.

Hardcover 978-1-4626-3599-3
Softcover 978-1-4626-3600-6
PUBLISHED BY PUBLISHAMERICA, LLLP
www.publishamerica.com
Baltimore

Printed in the United States of America

Chapter 1.

The campaign was reaching it's climax. This election had been more exciting than any that the long-time residents of Eversleigh could remember. There were more candidates for Council positions than ever before and it had been a noisy few weeks with a lot of sharp verbal attacks, especially against the Mayor and some of the Councillors who had completed their term and were running for re-election.

The issue of the proposed new industrial park had created rumblings in the community throughout the year but had reached boiling point in the rhetoric of this election. It was an issue that had split the town in two and was the main reason for the large number of people running for office and the expectation of a high voter turnout on election day.

"A new industrial park is vital to the future of Eversleigh." These words were uttered with passion by Dick Barrett at the last public meeting before the election. His next sentence was lost in conflicting shouts. "No, never!" yelled half the crowd, while cheers of approval rang out from the rest. No one was neutral.

This was Dick's first venture into municipal politics and he was going for the top position. He was challenging the incumbent mayor, Jim Stevens, and the creation of a new industrial park was the issue that sharply divided the two men. It was the issue that had prompted Dick to get involved. Although he was a new candidate he was not new to the town. As a partner in a successful and long-established real estate business, he was well known and well liked in the community in which he had been born and in which he had spent his whole life.

For the past three years Dick had been a member of the special steering committee investigating the proposal to bring new industry to the town. During that time he had learned a great deal about the importance of the need to create more employment opportunities that would maintain the economic stability of the small town. A site had been chosen for a proposed industrial park, and an application for development funding for the project was being sent to the Province. The pros and cons of the issue had been debated endlessly in the letters to the editor column of the local paper, and now the battle lines were drawn in the arena of the municipal election.

Not all the opponents to the proposal were old time residents of the town who wanted their townl to remain the quiet peaceful place it had always been. In recent years a number of people had moved to Eversleigh, many of them to find an attractive place to spend their retirement years. Quite a few of them had come from the cities across Southern Ontario— Toronto, Hamilton, Kitchener, London and Windsor. These were people who were tired of the stress of city life and were looking for some place that was less hectic.

Typical of this group of newcomers was Fred Neilson, an industrial engineer with an office in a high rise building in the downtown core of the city, just over an hour's drive away. He had lived in Eversleigh only three years. He liked the town. It hadn't taken him long to get involved in community activities, and now he was a candidate for council.

"This town has charm. It has beauty. It's a pleasure to come home from the city each night to this place," he proclaimed. He had bought a hundred year old yellow brick home in the oldest part of the town, and he looked forward to the day, not too far away now, when he would be able to retire and devote himself even more fully to keeping the community alive and vibrant. He had participated actively in the campaign to build the library extension. He saw a library as an important asset to the town. But he was adamantly opposed to any plan to bring new industry into the town. To his way of thinking that would destroy all that was appealing about this town. He had run a good campaign and he thought that even though he was a relative newcomer, he had a good chance of being elected to council.

For Cathy Silcox this election was an exciting new experience. She was the branch librarian at the Eversleigh Public Library. She knew most people in town from their visits to the library, and they knew her. Particularly over the past year, during which a major physical expansion of the library had been completed, she had had the opportunity to meet with many of the leaders of the community to discuss the expansion plans and the fundraising program which had been wildly successful. She had decided that she would be a candidate for the town council, and she thought she had a chance to win. She had enjoyed the campaign, but as election day drew nearer she was nervous. She was unsure about the outcome of the vote, and she began to question whether she really did have what it would take to be an effective councillor.

As the crowd poured out of the hall at the end of the final all candidates meeting Joe Simmons waited for Cathy. Joe was the principal of the District High School, and an ardent supporter of Cathy's. In fact, he d helped design her campaign leaflet and had personally knocked on many doors seeking support for her candidacy. His tall athletic build, handsome features and a natural smile made him as popular with most of the parents as he was with his students.

"Fantastic, Cathy!" he said as she came down the steps and they turned north up Main Street together. "You've certainly set this town on fire. You've rocked it to its foundation. However the vote goes on Monday, the town will never be the same again."

"Oh, come on Joe, don't exaggerate like that!" laughed Cathy. "You know it's the issues that are going to have an effect on the town's future, not me or for that matter any one single candidate. But tell me seriously, did I really do alright tonight?" She pulled up the big collar on her coat as a shield against the biting wind. "I had an awful fit of jitters up there on the stage. It seems I get more nervous every time I get up to speak. I have this weird feeling that I'm some kind of imposter. And then when I get all that applause, I feel that I really must be among friends. You know how it feels when you have a fever? You keep getting hot all over—then you shiver—then you're burning hot again. I can't wait until Monday night and it will all be over."

"And then you'll be Councillor Silcox, and I'll just be one of your subjects," laughed Joe.

"Don't be silly, Joe. Are you coming up for a drink?" They had reached the small apartment building where Cathy lived.

"Just one drink to unwind from all that excitement," said Joe. "But I mustn't stay long. I need an early night."

Cathy took a bottle of Labbatt's Blue from the fridge for Joe, and poured herself a Coke. She dropped some ice in the Coke, opened the beer and took them through to the living room where Joe was already sprawled comfortably in one of the two big arm chairs. She slipped her feet out of her shoes and tucked them under her in her favourite position in the other chair. She lit a cigarette, threw her head back and blew a long cloud of smoke to the ceiling.

"You smoke too much, Cathy," said Joe. "It's not good for you."

"I know. I know. But it sure calms the nerves. It helps me to think, too. I keep telling myself I should stop. Every time I see one of those commercials the health people put out, I cringe. But it's the only little vice I've got. And it won't give me a pot belly like all that beer you drink!"

Cathy was an attractive young woman in her early thirties. Her long naturally blonde hair and deep blue eyes attracted attention wherever she went. Her figure had all the dimensions which other women tortured themselves to achieve. She could have had her pick of male friends in any community. But Cathy's whole life was motivated by two driving ambitions, and male friends didn't have a place in either one. At least not until very recently. One of the side effects of the election campaign seemed to be that she was spending rather a lot of time with Joe Simmons. But, as she would consciously remind herself every so often, "There's nothing personal about this—he's just a good campaign supporter, and I value his advice."

Her first ambition was related to her job as librarian. She was dedicated to the task of upgrading library services and making the public aware of the great advances that have transformed libraries into modern resource centres, making use of every type of audio-visual technique as well as the newest in computer and internet technology. The recent expansion to the library had given new impetus to this challenge.

Her second ambition was to propagate as effectively as she could the awareness that women have the same rights as men. Although many people thought this was a battle that had been fought and won twenty years ago, Cathy knew that there were still a lot of deep-rooted prejudices about the place of women in society. Although it was not her style to march in placard-waving protests organized by feminist groups, she had a lot of friends in what is still called "the women's movement". Her approach, however, was less flamboyant, quieter and she felt more pragmatic. She was simply determined to show by her personal example that she was the equal of any man. She knew that she possessed leadership skills and she was not prepared to take second place to anyone on the basis of gender.

Joe Simmons was thirty five, and had been Principal of the High School for less than a year. He was no stranger to Eversleigh, however. He came here to teach English and Phys. Ed. following graduation eleven years ago. Four years later, when he was appointed head of the English Department he married Sharon Scott, daughter of the Anglican Rector. A year later, when they were expecting their first child, Sharon was killed in a head-on collision south of town during a heavy snow storm. Joe kept his grief to himself, and became a very private person. He was an excellent teacher, and had a good rapport with his students, but away from school he led a quiet and uninvolved life, except for a recent interest in the plans to create an industrial park . He had become a member of the steering committee that also included members of town council and local business people. He had been appointed secretary of the committee.

After a spell as Vice Principal of the High School, he was appointed Principal last year. It was his involvement with the proposed industrial park that generated his interest in municipal politics, for it had given him a greater awareness of how the various groups of citizens interacted with each other, and the hidden agendas that were so often the impetus for decision making. He had also become aware that if town council was not in favour of any proposed new development, that proposal would have a rough road to becoming reality.

It was therefore with a new interest that Joe evaluated the candidates for election to Council this year. In the process of this evaluation he came to know Cathy Silcox.

A mutual admiration and friendship developed over the few weeks that they had worked closely together on the campaign. As they sat in the big arm chairs and weighed up the prospects of victory next Monday, it occurred to Joe that he hadn't been alone with a woman like this since Sharon was killed six years ago. He immediately dismissed the thought, reminding himself that this was a political campaign, not a budding romance. However, he couldn't completely banish the stirring in his groin that had been ignited by his stray thought.

"I must go, Cathy". He drained the second beer. "I need my beauty sleep."

Cathy unwound her legs from under her body, and helped Joe into his coat.

"I doubt if I'll sleep all week-end," she said "no matter what happens to my beauty."

"That's one thing you don't have to worry about," said Joe as he opened the front door. He turned, and on impulse gave her a light kiss on the cheek. "Good luck!"

She stood with one hand on the door and rubbed her cheek with the other hand as she listened to his footsteps going downstairs, and the sound of outside door slamming shut.

Back in the big arm chair with her feet tucked under her, she looked across at the empty chair.

"Well, I'll be damned!" she said aloud.

Chapter 2.

Election day dawned. The weather was clear, and although the temperature was no higher than could be expected on a late Fall say in Ontario, the sun shone brightly all day. The turn out at the polls was heavy, and when the counting of ballots began in the big room at the town hall, there was an overflow crowd on hand.

"Looks like this one's going to be a close race to the end, Tom," said Mayor Jim Stevens.

The mayor had expected an easy victory when the campaign began. But the intensity of Dick Barrett's campaign and the uncertainty of just how much support the industrial park proposal had, combined to make Stevens uneasy. It was only in the last week that he recognized the possibility that he might lose this election.

"That's right, Jim," replied Tom Hillman. "I don't know whether either of us are going to be re-elected this time."

"It looks like the girl might make it."

As he spoke, the Mayor looked up at the latest chalk figures on the blackboard. In addition to the race for mayor, there were six councillors to be elected. The vote count now showed that four of these were safely elected. The tally of votes for the next three candidates, Cathy Silcox, Tom Hillman and Fred Neilson, mounted at an almost identical rate. But only two of them would be elected. Although Cathy and Fred were first time candidates, Tom Hillman had been on Council for twelve years.

Eighty excited gasps became one single roar as the new figures on the chalk board indicated another change. Jim Stevens had now overtaken the early lead of newcomer Dick Barrett in the contest for Mayor.

"Don't worry about that, Dick," whispered his wife, Susan. "Those last votes came from the poll where Jim lives. You'd expect him to be strong there."

"I know. But this neck and neck fight to the finish is hard on the nerves.". The temperature in the room was rising. The heat generated by eighty bodies and the constant excited chatter all added to the atmosphere of suspense as the last few polling stations reported their results. Another roar went up from the crowd. This time the swing was the other way. These votes had come from the new subdivision. They had been heavily in favour of Barrett, and he was now in the lead again.

In the other race, there were ten candidates for the six Council seats. Soon after the polls closed, it had been apparent that three of the candidates had not secured enough support to be elected. With each new tally, they trailed further behind. This left seven serious contenders for the six seats. The four leading candidates were assured of election early in the evening, but the fifth and sixth seats were still a toss-up between Silcox, Neilson and Hillman. The count was slower in this part of the election process as votes still had to be tallied for all ten candidates.

The election of the Mayor would be decided on the next count. The town administrator's pretty young assistant went to the blackboard again, paper in one hand, chalk in the other. There was a sudden silence as she began to write the final tally Barrett 1,543 Stevens 1,469.

This time the roar was deafening. It was also prolonged. One of the first to reach Dick Barrett to shake his hand was the defeated Mayor, Jim Stevens.

"Congratulations, Dick," he said. "It was a clean fight."

"Thanks Jim."

In the other election the counting continued. The crowd waited for the next chalk tally to be added to the board. Cathy stood in a corner of the crowded room surrounded by a dedicated group of supporters including Joe Simmons and Sally Redfern. Sally was Cathy's assistant at the library and had devoted all her spare time to the campaign in recent weeks in addition to carrying an extra load in the library while Cathy was on the hustings. She stood beside her candidate now, hardly daring to breathe.

"I can't bear the suspense," whispered Sally.

"You can't?" said Cathy. "What do you think it's doing to me?"

With only one more polling station to report, Cathy had a nine vote lead. That last report could swing it the other way.

"That poll is one I visited myself," said Joe. "I'm sure you'll take it. You've won, Cathy! You've won!"

"Be quiet, Joe. I'm not there until the vote's in. You're making me nervous. Wouldn't it be awful if I cry, and act like a woman," she added with a laugh. Silence descended once again on the crowd. The final tally was ready. The numbers were posted alphabetically.

Hillman 495

Neilson 483

Silcox 504

The silence was shattered. The crowd roared. The twelve year veteran, Tom Hillman, had retained his seat and newcomer Cathy Silcox would take her seat beside him at the Council table.

A mist swam before her eyes. She was crying! Tears of relief—tears of joy—she fought them back as the crowd surged around her, pumping her hand in congratulation. Sally hugged her, and even Joe cast his usual reticence aside and kissed her full on the lips.

"You made it, Councillor," he yelled in her ear as the flash of photographers' camer blinded her through the mist.

As the noise subsided, Fred Neilson moved through the crowd and reached out his hand as he said with a smile— "Congratulations, Cathy! You deserved to win."

"Come on, Cathy," said Joe. "There's a party planned at my place. Let's go, or your friends will drink all the champagne before we get there."

Cathy, Joe and Sally together with a dozen or so jubilant supporters set out in high spirits to Joe's house. They had gone two blocks before Cathy realized that she had her arm tucked naturally through Joe's.

Joe had re-arranged the furniture in the front room, brought extra chairs over from the High School, and stocked his bar in anticipation of this celebration. And to Cathy's astonishment he really did have champagne.

The revelry continued into the early hours of the morning, and as the last guests departed Joe got his coat and told Cathy he'd walk her home. For someone who normally restricted her drinking to straight Cokes the unfamiliar potency of the champagne, combined with the excitement of the occasion to generate a strange "walking-on-air" sensation. This time it was necessary to hang on to Joe's arm just to keep her feet on the ground!

At the front door of Cathy's building Joe turned towards her and taking her into his arms gave her a long lingering kiss. As their lips parted, she whispered "Thank you, Joe. Thank you for everything." Then she turned, let herself in, and floated upstairs to her apartment.

Chapter 3.

The big clock on the wall of the council chamber struck six.

"Harry, give Dick a call, will you," said Tom Hillman, one of the few returning Councillors, with a touch of impatience in his voice. "We've got to get this show on the road, and we can't start without him. I hope this isn't a sign of the way things are going to be run this year."

All members of Council were in their places at the appointed hour except for the newly elected mayor. The big chair at the head of the Council table remained empty awaiting his arrival.

Of the seven people elected, three of them were former incumbents. They had been through this inaugural ceremony before. The three newly elected members in addition to Dick Barrett, the new mayor, were Cathy Silcox, Dan Simpson, a pharmacist, and Derek Wheeler, the manager of the Royal Bank.

The inaugural meeting of a new Council is largely a ceremonial affair, with little or no regular business being transacted. The oath of office is administered to each member of Council by the town administrator. The Mayor delivers his inaugural address outlining his hopes and plans for the coming year. The meeting then adjourns, and everyone goes to the Legion Hall for the inaugural reception.

Harry McLaughlin, the town administrator, went out of the council chamber without a word. Harry was a man of few words. He never used them unnecessarily. But he had a head full of facts. Council members had relied heavily on him for the past ten years. He could be heard now using the telephone across the hall. Conversation died out in the council chamber. Everyone was anxious to get the preliminaries out of the way. Harry returned and announced "Better begin without him. Susan says he wasn't going home before the meeting. There's no reply at his office. Must have been called out on business. I can administer the oath to him later." For Harry that was a long speech.

"We can't start without the mayor," complained Tom Hillman.

"Well we can't sit here all night waiting for him. Like Harry says, he can administer the oath to him when he gets here. Teach him not to be late again!" growled George Mitchell, another veteran councillor.

In the uneasy atmosphere the oaths were administered and the basic formalities conducted. The usual inaugural speeches were left to be made at the first regular council meeting and the meeting was adjourned.

"Not much to report there," thought Jack Porter at the small table in the corner reserved for the press. Jack had covered Council meetings for the Star, Eversleigh's weekly newspaper, for seven years. He had never got much news out of any inaugural meeting. At least the absence of the new mayor would be worth a couple of lines.

"Dick hasn't gone too far," said Cathy as they left the building to go to the reception. "His car is parked in its usual place."

Barrett's office was directly across the street from the Town Hall, immediately adjacent to the site on which the new medical clinic was being built. The excavation work had already begun, and Barrett had complained to everyone that he couldn't hear himself think in his office now.

"He knows where to find us. He'll probably join us before the reception's over," said Tom Hillman as they walked up the street.

Derek Wheeler was the first to leave after the reception. He was treasurer of the hospital board, and a good friend of Barrett's. He walked back towards the town hall and glanced across the street at the real estate office. He noticed Dick's car was still there.

"That's strange," he thought. "It's not like Dick to miss something like tonight's meeting".

He made a sudden decision. He strode over and tried the door. It opened at his touch, and he walked into the brightly lit general office. Everything was as it should be. The computer was turned off. So was the photo copier. The desk tops were clean and the office had been left as any good secretary would be expected to leave it, except that the door was unlocked and the lights were on.

On the far wall there were two doors which Derek knew opened into the private offices of the firm's partners. With only a moment's uneasy hesitation he went around the front counter, past the filing cabinet and knocked on the door marked "R. J. Barrett". There was no sound. He turned the handle and swung the door inwards.

The light was on, and Dick was seated in the swivel chair behind his desk. His head and shoulders lay across the desk and a dark sticky pool overflowed from the blotter onto the shiny polished surface.

"Oh my God!" exclaimed Derek as he took in the sight before him. He took three quick steps across the floor and lifted Dick's hand. Knowing he was too late to help his friend, he dropped the hand back on the desk and stared in horror at the lifeless body. He knew that Dick Barrett was never going to occupy the mayor's leather chair that awaited him in the Council chamber across the street.

Chapter 4.

Jack Porter sat at his computer at the Star's office typing with remarkable speed. He smiled to himself as he recalled his thought of the previous evening that the absence of a new mayor might be worth a couple of lines. Now this absence was going to make the whole front page.

He had talked to some of the Councillors last night and now he began to transcribe their dazed comments—

"I can't believe it. Nothing like this has ever happened in this town".

"Not Dick Barrett! Nobody would do a thing like that to him!"

"What the hell is the world coming to?"

"I hope they get the bastard!"

Jack had never been this close to a murder before. As he typed their words he began to wonder if one of them was the murderer. Somebody must have done it. But who? And why? As he asked himself these questions—questions to which of course he could provide no answers—the thought flashed into his mind "Maybe I could do a little sleuthing myself. What a scoop if I solved the mystery!"

He soon abandoned this thought, reminding himself that it was his job to write the news, not to make it. That very fact meant that he would have to stay pretty close to the investigation that was already being organized. For the next few days reporters from the city dailies, the radio and TV stations and networks would be in town. But he had the inside track. He had been on the spot (or almost) and he knew everyone in town. Yes, for once he had an edge over the mass media types.

* * * * * * * *

Detective Inspector George Perkins of the Ontario Provincial Police was a big man. Six foot three inches tall with shoulders to make his height seem natural, Perkins had the ability to make the importance and authority of his presence appear to be perfectly in proportion with his physical size. The small, simply furnished office of Eversleigh's Police Chief seemed totally inadequate to contain his presence. His colleague, Detective Sergeant Bill Gordon, was a smaller, less conspicuous man, but one who was building a reputation on the force for his close attention to detail.

Chief Carl Montmore was more than a little uneasy as he sat on the edge of his chair. He had difficulty reminding himself that this was his office and that these two men were his guests in a sense. What he didn't realize was that many men of greater stature than himself had felt the same inadequacy in the presence of George Perkins.

His uneasiness was not relieved by his awareness that one of the issues the new council would have to deal with was the proposal to shut down the local town police force and turn everything over to the Ontario Provincial Police. This suggestion had been shelved by last year's council, but would inevitably be back on the agenda before long. The fact that the Provincial Police had to be involved in this investigation didn't help the Chief to feel confident about the future. In all his years as Chief this was the first murder in Eversleigh. The small local force was able to deal effectively with the normal round of domestic disturbances, juvenile delinquency, the occasional drunken brawl, auto theft and break and enter cases. But he knew that neither he nor his officers had the expertise or the equipment to handle a murder investigation.

"We have a full hour in which the shooting could have taken place," Perkins was saying. "Barrett's secretary says that he was alive at five o'clock when she left the office. She's quite definite that she spoke to him face to face just before she left, and that he planned to finish up his work and come straight over here for the Council meeting. He should have been here by six o'clock or a little earlier. McLaughlin phoned his office at ten after six and got no reply. The doctor's report can't narrow it down any further, so we'll have to check a lot of people's movements during that time period. That'll be your job, Bill. See if you can find a witness who saw anyone entering or leaving Barrett's office after five o'clock. The main office door opens onto Main Street and there must have been a lot of people about at that time. For one thing, all the councillors would have been arriving here. Check them out, of course, and see if you can find out who was on the street between five and six. The problem is that there's a side door from the alley which goes directly into Barrett's private office. That door wasn't locked, and the chances are that the murderer came in that way. Not too many people would have seen a person using the alley. You'd better check with the construction workers on that clinic building site. They didn't leave until five thirty, I'm told. And the back door of the clinic opens onto the far end of that alley."

"O.K., sir, I'll start making enquiries," responded the sergeant. "There doesn't seem to be any kind of motive in the affair that would narrow things down a bit, does there?"

"There's no sign of any yet," said Perkins. "Robbery doesn't seem to have been involved—at least there's no suggestion yet that anything was taken from the office. As far as we know at this point nobody obviously benefits from Barrett's death, but we'll have to check further into that. Of course, he'd been involved in a pretty fierce election campaign and might have made some enemies that way. But political murders aren't too common in this country. I'll do some work on the motive angle. Maybe the Chief can give me some leads, and I'll have to go and talk to the widow. You'd better get started on your leg work, Bill, and keep your ears to the ground. There's not much that goes unnoticed in a town of this size."

"O.K., sir," replied the detective again as he moved to the door. "I'll see you later."

"There's one more thing," added the Inspector. "There was no sign of the gun at the scene. We should have a report in a day or two on what kind of gun we're looking for, but in the meantime we'll see if the Chief can put together a list of people who own guns in town."

Carl Montmore's sense of confidence was still at a low ebb. The Inspector's remark that he might be able to provide some ideas about a motive had not made him feel better. Hadn't he sat up all night torturing himself with this question. "Why? Why? Why? Why Dick Barrett?"

Of all the town residents surely Dick Barrett was at the top of the list as far as the size and scope of his circle of friends was concerned. He had a reputation for scrupulous honesty and fair dealing in business, even when it cost him money. Dick had no enemies. Even his opponents in an election campaign that had evoked many bitter charges, had nothing but respect for Dick. The first important question the O.P.P. Inspector was going to ask him was a question for which he would have no answer. He could think of no motive for this crime.

Chapter 5.

Entering the town library, Sergeant Gordon approached the young woman behind the counter. "Is Miss Silcox in?" he asked,

"I'll see if she's free. What name shall I tell her?"

"I'm Sergeant Gordon of the O.P.P.," he replied.

She knocked on a door in the corner of the library and went in. She returned immediately. "Cathy will be right with you," she informed him.

The door opened again and another young woman came towards him. She put out her hand and smiled. "Good morning, sergeant. I'm Cathy Silcox. Please come in." The office was small and cramped, and in fact she spent very little time in it. There was just room for a small desk with a swivel desk chair behind it and two small chairs in front. She closed the door and invited him to sit. Rather than taking the chair behind the desk she hoisted herself onto the front corner of the desk and crossed her legs.

Although he was a happily married man, Bill Gordon appreciated attractive women. He had to admit that he had rarely seen a more attractive woman than this. The trim figure in the white blouse with all the curves in just the right place, the short black skirt which showed to advantage a pair of perfectly shaped legs, the long blonde hair and the deep blue eyes all combined to shatter the detective's pre-conceived ideas of what a feminist was supposed to look like.

He had already gained the information that the librarian was known in town as a feminist. He freely admitted that he didn't understand the feminist movement. He couldn't see why women wanted to be the same as men, why they wanted men's jobs, wanted to be policemen, firemen and bus drivers. On the few occasions he had given any serious thought to the matter, he had reached the conclusion that those who espoused this cause must be frustrated, plain-looking women who were destined to remain spinsters because they held no attraction for men. In their frustration at being denied the full role intended for women, they found escape in the unnatural claims of the feminist movement. He was therefore quite unprepared for Cathy Silcox. He made a mental note that before this case was over he was going to find out more about this feminist business. But being a conscientious man, work must come first.

"Miss Silcox," he began "I understand you were at the Council meeting last night, and were present when the murder of Mr. Barrett was discovered. I am hoping that you may be able to assist us in our investigation."

"Yes, I was at the meeting. But if you want to be completely accurate, I wasn't present when the body was discovered. After the meeting we all went to a reception at the Legion Hall. Derek Wheeler was the first to leave. A few minutes later, as the rest of us were putting on our coats, he ran back into the hall with the news of the murder. Quite frankly, I haven't thought of anything else since that time, but my thoughts have produced no results. So I'm afraid there really isn't anything I can tell you."

"Leave it to me to decide what's important," responded the detective. "You may be able to tell us more than you think. You see, this business of crime detection is really a scientific process. We gather a vast number of small, seemingly unimportant details. We set them down side by side and scrutinize them until one of them doesn't match up with the others. Then we have something to work with. My job at this point is to get as many of the facts as possible. Perhaps I can start by asking you two or three specific questions. What time did you leave the library last night? What were your movements between that time and your arrival at the Town Hall? And in particular, did you notice anyone entering or leaving Mr. Barrett's office?

"Oh, I get it," smiled Cathy. "You want to know if I have an alibi for the time the shot was fired, and if not then you'll start asking about my motives." She said this with a mischievous twinkle in her eye. "I hate to disappoint you, but I think I have a cast-iron alibi. Of course, I know that all murderers make sure they have one, so maybe it won't help me. But here goes anyway.

"I was here in the library until about five thirty five on Wednesday. We close at five thirty and my assistant, Sally Redfern, left promptly at that time. But Joe Simmons was here. He's the principal of the High School, and he's very anxious to make some improvements in the school library. He had stopped by to pick my brains about this. He arrived just before five o'clock.

"Joe walked with me to the Town Hall. Actually, we stopped in at the post office. They close at five-forty-five, you know. We both had some mail to dispose of and I bought some stamps. As we arrived at the Town Hall Tom Hillman came up the street from the other direction—he's another member of council and he runs a men's wear store in the next block".

She paused to bring the scene back into her memory.

"The three of us stood chatting for a few minutes and then Tom and I went into the Town Hall. That was about ten minutes to six. So you see, I can vouch for my movements all evening."

"While you were standing outside the Town Hall did you happen to see anyone going in or out of the real estate office across the street?"

"No, I'm afraid not. We were too deep in conversation about the proposed industrial park to be watching the comings and goings of anyone else. I know that sounds as though I must be very unobservant, but that's the way it was."

She did not share with the sergeant the fact that recently when she was with Joe she hardly ever noticed the comings and goings of other folk!

She sat back in her chair and picked up a pack of cigarettes from her desk. "Do you mind if I smoke?" she asked. "I know it's a bad habit, and the library itself is a no smoking area, but I make an exception in the office. It helps me to think. At least that's my excuse. Can I offer you one?"

"No thanks," said the detective. "But go ahead. It won't bother me".

He made a few notes in a small pocket-sized note book. "Thank you, Miss Silcox. If everyone could be that explicit our job would be much easier. I may be back again with some more questions as things develop".

As he stood up, another thought occurred to him. "I believe the recent election campaign was quite a lively affair. You must have seen and heard quite a bit of the other candidates in the past few weeks. Do you know of any enemies that Dick Barrett might have made?"

"Enemies? Dick?" Cathy looked surprised. "No. Although it was a lively campaign, it was pretty clean. There was very little mud-slinging, and I would say none was thrown Dick's way. He was respected by everyone, even his opponents. I can't imagine him having enemies."

"And yet," mused Gordon "someone shot him to death. And that someone must have had a pretty compelling reason. It wasn't an accident. Well, thank you for your time, Miss Silcox. And thank you for being so co-operative. If you think of anything that might have any bearing on this matter, you'll let me know, won't you?"

After she had walked to the front door of the library with the detective, Cathy returned to the office. She went over in her mind the conversation she had just shared, and her thoughts began to parallel those of Jack Porter in the Star Office a little earlier. As with the newsman, the thought came to Cathy—"Maybe I could do a little sleuthing myself." She had a naturally enquiring mind. She enjoyed searching through old volumes for facts needed by someone to support a thesis. She liked Bill Gordon's description of detective work. How did he put it? "A scientific process of gathering a vast number of small, seemingly unimportant details, setting them down side by side, scrutinizing them until one of them doesn't match up with the others." Yes, she liked that. And she did have one big advantage. Her campaign had been a very personal one. She had knocked on every door in Eversleigh. She knew a lot of people now, and she knew a great deal about them. She decided to apply herself to the challenging task of solving Dick Barrett's murder. Having made this decision Cathy had a momentary feeling that perhaps she'd better back off. After all, she did have a full time job and she had spent a lot of time away from the library during the campaign. And of course her new responsibilities on Council would probably be quite time-consuming. She really couldn't spare the time to play detective.

These doubts, however, were short lived. The sleuthing would be strictly a spare time diversion. She'd talk to Joe about it and they could work on it together. She'd make sure that the library got first priority on her time. But it would be exciting to solve a real murder case, or even help in solving it. If she did uncover any real clues she'd have to turn them over to Sergeant Gordon, of course. Having made a valiant effort to satisfy her conscience she got down to work and concentrated on her job for the rest of the day.

Chapter 6.

Inspector Perkins parked his car in the street outside the attractive two story brick home. It had a cared-for look about it, evident not only in the condition of the building, but also in the landscaping.

In response to his finger on the bell push he heard the melodic chimes inside the house. The door was opened by a slightly built woman in her early thirties. She had short dark hair and brown eyes. It was evident from those eyes that she had been crying recently, but she smiled at the Inspector.

"Good morning!"

"Good morning, madame! I'm Inspector Perkins. You are Mrs. Barrett?"

"Yes, I'm Susan Barrett. Please come in". She opened the door wider, and led him into a large, tastefully furnished living room opening off the spacious hallway.

The room ran the full length of the house with a window overlooking the road and the front as well as a large picture window overlooking the landscaped rear garden.

When they were seated, the Inspector said "I'm sorry I have to bother you so soon with a lot of questions at this time, Mrs. Barrett, but I assure you that it's absolutely necessary."

His expression of sorrow was not a glib phrase. In all his years on the force he still dreaded the interview with the widowed spouse of a murder victim.

"I understand, Inspector. You have a job to do that's not easy. I'll help you any way I can. I've got over the first shock now, but it's still hard to believe that it really happened."

"I'm sure it is. Tell me, do you have any idea why someone might have wanted to harm your husband?"

Despite her assertion that she had got over the first shock, it was apparent that she was in deep distress. Tears began to roll down her cheeks. She dabbed at them with a handkerchief before she replied.

"No, I'm at a complete loss. I just can't understand it. He lived here all his life and everyone knew him. He was a very likeable person. We've both lived here all our lives. We both went to High School here. That's where I met Dick. In fact, I teach at the same school now".

She was having no success in keeping back the tears and had to dab at her eyes again with the handkerchief she was gripping in her tightly clenched fist.

"We have so many friends in town that we have known so long. Everybody knew Dick, and they all liked him".

"That's no different to what I've heard from others," said Perkins. "He does seem to have been respected by most people in town, which makes it all the more difficult to find a motive for his death. Let me ask you another question. Did your husband say anything, or give you any kind of indication that made you think he was worried?"

There was an uneasy pause before he got an answer.

"It's hard to be sure, Inspector. Yes, I think there was something. He's been rather withdrawn for two or three weeks now."

"Did he give you any reason for this?"

"No. When I mentioned it, he just said everything was fine—but it wasn't. Something's been bothering him."

"He didn't give you any hint at all whether it had anything to do with the recent election—or perhaps some problem at work?"

Again she was slow to answer the question. Instead she got up from the chair in which she had been gently rocking herself, and walked over to the big picture window. She stood in silence for a while staring out of the window. Then without turning around she said, "No, it wasn't the election. He enjoyed the campaign. He talked about it a lot, and he was thrilled by all the votes he got. He was looking forward to serving as mayor."

She paused again, but Perkins didn't interrupt. Still looking through the window, she went on, "And I'm sure it wasn't his work. It kept him in touch with people all the time, and he loved people. He really got himself involved with the decisions his clients made when they bought a house or a farm. He knew that was a big thing in their lives, and he tried to put himself in their shoes and see all the pros and cons. That's why he was so good at his work. It was more than a job to him. It was his life, and he'd come home and tell me about it every night. He'd tell me about the people he met, and what they thought about the various properties. I felt part of it too."

There was another silence, and then she turned to face him. The Inspector knew before she turned around that she had given up trying to stem the tears which now flowed unhindered down her cheeks.

"We were very much in love, Inspector. We haven't been blessed with children, but we really share each other's lives. Oh God!" she exclaimed. "Please excuse me for a few minutes, Inspector."

She moved out of the room and across the hall into the bathroom.

The Inspector knew that this hurt was going to take a long time to heal.

When she returned she had regained her earlier composure, and she seated herself once more in the rocker. She had obviously made a decision.

"Inspector Perkins," she began, "I don't know whether this will help you or not. You'll have to judge for yourself. I was telling you the truth when I said I didn't know what was worrying Dick, but I think I know when it began. About three weeks ago he went to a special meeting about the industrial park that has been proposed. It must have gone on very late because I was asleep when he got home, and I didn't go to bed until after the eleven o'clock news. Next morning he was very quiet. He wouldn't tell me anything about the meeting, and from then on he was obviously worried about something— something he wouldn't share with me. And that wasn't like Dick."

Chapter 7.

"An older house with a bit of character about it, if you can find one." Cathy Silcox sat across the desk from Ken Davey in the real estate office. She tried not to think that Dick had been murdered in the next room. "I'm not too keen on those square boxes they're building in the subdivisions. They're like cereal cartons on a supermarket shelf—all the same, no individuality. Tiny rooms. I might as well stay in my apartment as buy one of those."

Cathy was not yet laying all her cards on the table. It was true that she had been thinking about buying a house, and it was also true that when she did take this step she would look for a place with some character, but the real reason she had come to see Davey was her decision to do a bit of amateur sleuthing.

If she intended to solve Dick Barrett's murder, she had to start as close to the scene of the crime as possible. She decided that his partner would be the most likely person to tell her more about Dick Barrett.

"That's easier said than done, Cathy," said Ken. "The old houses don't come on the market too often. And they don't stay empty for long."

"I can believe that. But I can wait until I see the right thing. Do you have anything at all you could show me now?"

"Two bedrooms?"

"Yes. I certainly don't need more than that. It would be nice to have a spare room when I have a friend up."

"Most of the older houses have four and five bedrooms. There's just one place I can think of with two: Old Miss McNaughton's place up at the North End. It's been empty a long time, but I doubt if it's what you're looking for. I'll show it to you if you like."

Cathy knew the house well, and wouldn't live in it under any circumstances, but she'd let him show her through the place before agreeing that it wasn't what she had in mind.

"Yes, I'd like that. Do you have time?"

"Sure. No problem." Ken took his coat from the hook on the back of the door and helped Cathy on with hers.

"We're going up to the McNaughton place, Debbie," he said to the secretary as they went through the outer office. "I won't be too long."

The house was, in fact, in even worse state than Cathy had expected. As they left the driveway and turned back towards town, Cathy said, "Ken, there's something else I want to talk about. Could we go some place for a coffee—somewhere we can talk?"

He looked at his watch. "It's quarter to twelve," he said. "Let's make it lunch?"

"All right!"

When they had ordered he asked her—"What's on your mind?"

She didn't answer immediately. She wasn't sure how blunt she dared be. "Ken, there's no easy way to put this. But I've got to find out who killed Dick." Her words startled him into silence.

She continued, "It's not just curiosity. Dick and I were just elected to Council. We were going to work together. He would have been a good mayor. But someone shut him up just before his first Council meeting. I don't think that was a coincidence. I want to know why he was killed."

"It's no use, Cathy. I can't help you. I've asked myself the same question, but there aren't any answers. It just doesn't make any sense."

Their conversation was interrupted by the arrival of the waitress. As they ate their lunch, Cathy asked a lot of questions about Dick Barrett.

"What things were important to him? What things frustrated him? What made him angry?"

"His work was important to him. He loved this business. And this town meant a lot to him. That's why he got involved in that committee for the industrial park. That's why he ran for mayor. He wanted to give something back to his community."

After a brief silence, he went on, "What frustrated him? What made him angry? People who weren't straight with him. People with hidden agendas. He was so bloody honest himself, that it made him angry when he saw dishonesty."

"Was he angry recently?"

"I don't know about angry. But I know he was worried. Something was bugging him. I think someone got under his skin at the last meeting of the industrial park committee."

"Did he tell you about it?"

"No. But ever since that meeting he's been brooding in a way that wasn't natural for him. God, I don't know whether that had anything to do with him being killed. I don't even know what it was all about."

It wasn't much, but it was a start, thought Cathy. She had been away from the library for much of the morning and once again she realized how grateful she was for the loyalty and the competence of Sally Redfern. She didn't leave the library all afternoon, but she did make one brief phone call to Joe Simmons. On the way home she stopped at Joe's house. He had the minutes of the last few meetings of the industrial park committee ready for her as he had promised he would.

"Come on in for a while," Joe invited her with a smile.

"No thanks, Joe. Not right now. I want to get home and get into something comfortable. I've got a lot of thinking to do. Thanks for the minutes."

After hanging up her heavy winter coat, Cathy went into her bedroom and took off her blouse and skirt, and put on a tee shirt and a pair of jeans. She made herself a cheese salad which she ate at the kitchen table while glancing at the newspaper. She followed the salad with a yogurt, and then curled herself up in her favourite position in one of the big arm chairs with her bare feet tucked under her. On the small table beside the chair she placed a tall glass of Coke, the file with the minutes Joe had given her, and her cigarettes and lighter.

She lit a cigarette, picked up the file and began to read the minutes with a feeling of excitement. The excitement soon gave way to puzzlement, and then to a sense of frustration.

"Bloody hell!" she said exclaimed aloud. "There must be something here I'm missing".

She went back to the beginning and started reading again, more slowly this time. The meeting in question had evidently been quite short and dealt with only one subject—the impact of the operating costs of the proposed industrial park on the town budget, and by extension on the increase that would be necessary in the tax rate. Although the companies that moved into the new buildings would pay rent, it would be necessary to offer incentives to them in the beginning. . So the town may be faced with high initial costs and perhaps higher annual operating costs than had originally been expected. The discussion had included some talk about the way in which the town's mill rate was set. That was all, except for an appendix which was in the form of a table showing a comparison of the town's present and projected tax revenue. But none of this seemed to be in any way sinister or a cause for alarm as far as Cathy could see. The meeting had adjourned at nine fifteen.

"There's nothing strange there," thought Cathy. "Something must have happened or something was said that didn't get into the minutes".

She put the file down, went to the fridge and refilled her glass with Coke. She lit another cigarette and as she did so she realized that she only had two left in the pack. She went back to her chair and tried to relate what Ken Davey had said to what she had read in the minutes.

Her thoughts were interrupted by the ring of the telephone.

"Hello! Cathy Silcox speaking."

"Cathy, it's Joe. Did you find what you wanted in those minutes?"

"Frankly, no I didn't. Joe, are you busy? Could you spare me half an hour or so? I'm as frustrated as hell, and I think you may be able to help me with something I'm trying to figure out."

"Sure. I'll be right over." Joe didn't need any persuading.

"Oh, and Joe," she just thought of something before he put the receiver down. "Stop in at the variety store would you, and get me a pack of cigarettes. I'm almost out."

"I don't know why I should encourage you in your bad habits," he laughed.

"Oh, don't be so damned self-righteous. Pick me up a pack of DuMaurier and I'll have a cold beer waiting for you when you get here."

"Feed each other's vices, eh? O.K."

* * * * * * * * * *

When they were settled in the big arm chairs Joe asked, "What's on your mind? Are you just doing homework for the next Council meeting, or are you looking for something specific?"

"There's something very specific. It's about Dick's murder."

"Dick's murder? What the hell do those minutes have to do with Dick's murder?"

"Shut up a minute and listen, Joe. I'm trying to get my thoughts straightened out. I don't know why Dick was murdered, but I can't get it out of my head that it was something to do with him being elected mayor."

"But…" interrupted Joe.

"I said shut up and listen," snapped Cathy. "I'm trying to think straight. I had a talk with Ken Davey today, and he told me Dick had been worried about something that happened at the last meeting of that committee. That's why I asked you for those minutes. But I've read them through twice and I can't find any clue there. I'm frustrated. Joe."

"That's because there's no clue there. That meeting was just a short straightforward business meeting. Nothing was said that could lead to murder. Nobody raised their voices. Nobody even disagreed with anyone else. I know. I was there. Ken Davey's imagining things. But putting all that aside, why are you getting so het up about who murdered Dick Barrett?"

"I just don't think it was a coincidence that Dick was murdered just before his first Council meeting. I think he knew something that someone didn't want him to know, and someone shut him up before he opened his mouth at Council. I want to know who that someone was, and dammit, I'm going to find out."

"Knock it off, Cathy. It's not your business, and I don't want you getting involved in a murder investigation."

Cathy's feet came from under her and hit the floor with a thud as she stood up, a deep angry flush covering her face.

"What do you mean—You don't want me getting involved? Who do you think you are?" She was shouting. "Since when have you owned me? Since when did I need your permission to do anything?"

Joe was taken aback at the violent reaction he had generated. He stood up and faced her, partly in an effort to regain his composure and partly in an effort to stem the flow of words from Cathy.

"Hold it! Hold it!" he finally broke in. "I didn't mean it like that! I'm sorry! Let's start again. Murder is a serious business. It's police business. It's not something for private citizens to meddle in. It's not just you. I don't think any of us should start playing detective."

The flush left Cathy's face, although she was obviously far from being appeased. She sat down, opened the new pack of DuMaurier and lit another cigarette.

Joe was pacing back and forth across the room. "I didn't mean to be aggressive. I wasn't trying to suggest that I have any control over what you do. Of course I don't. But I care about you. Damn it, Cathy" he stopped pacing and turned to face her. "Damn it, Cathy. I love you!"

The last three words took her completely by surprise despite the preamble. She inhaled deeply, put her head back on the cushion and slowly blew a long cloud of smoke to the ceiling. Still looking at the smoke as it dispersed, she said in a much quieter tone—"That's the classiest retreat I've ever heard!" She looked at him with the hint of a smile coming back to her lips.

"My God, Cathy, you're impossible!" he exclaimed. "I said I love you, and I meant it. And anyway it doesn't really matter what I think about your aspirations to become a detective because I hear the police have got the case pretty well solved."

Cathy sat bolt upright. "What do you mean by that?" she demanded.

"I heard it at the barber shop this afternoon. They've found the murder weapon, and it sounds like they're going to make an arrest tomorrow."

"Who said that?"

"Oh you know how it is. The guys at the barber shop know everything."

Chapter 8.

"Well, Carl, I think we've got your man. Gordon's out checking to see if the time element fits". "He looks as though he'd like to add `It was elementary, my dear Watson'" thought Carl Montmore as Inspector Perkins smiled with confidence.

"It's definitely the murder weapon" said the Inspector. "The ballistics boys agree on that. It was dug up by the construction crew on the site of the medical clinic. No fingerprints on it, but it's registered in the name of Frederick Neilson".

The local police chief couldn't accept these blunt facts without protest. "But Neilson's not that kind of man, George. He's a family man. He's a good man. I know him personally. He's not a cold-blooded murderer".

The O.P.P. may have their technical know-how and all their scientific aids, but to Carl Montmore being a policemen in a small town meant knowing people. He prided himself on knowing the people of Eversleigh.

Fred Neilson had lived in town with his wife Jill and their three school-age children for only three years. In that time he had become active in the community. He coached a pee-wee hockey team, sang in the choir at the United Church, and was always ready to help with a worthwhile community project. His obvious sincerity combined with his natural talent for leadership, had already brought him the presidency of the Lions' Club. This was a remarkable achievement for such a recent `foreigner' in town. Could this man be a murderer?

The big Inspector's tone softened. "Listen, Carl. I know as well as you do that in police work we've got to find out what makes people tick. It's not just a matter of fingerprints and alibis and ballistics. You say you know Neilson. How well do you know him? Do you know why he came to Eversleigh? Do you know why he drives two hundred kilometres round trip to work every day?"

Montmore was damned if he could see the point in these questions.

The Inspector continued "Bill Gordon's a great man for detail. Since we traced the gun to Neilson yesterday, he's done a lot of work. He's been checking Neilson's background. He's talked to the man himself. Did you know that Neilson spent his boyhood in a none-too-prosperous neighbourhood on the near East side of Windsor—just a block from the Detroit River? His parents spent most of their time in the hotel at the corner of the street. Young Fred hated that life and was determined to get out. He worked and studied hard. He worked his way to a degree in industrial engineering".

"So what?" muttered the chief. "What the hell does all that have to do with Barrett's murder?"

"Once he got a good paying job" continued the Inspector, ignoring the interruption "his greatest ambition was to give his sons the kind of environment to grow up in which had been denied to him. That's why he moved to Eversleigh. That's why he didn't mind that round trip drive to the plant every day. That was also the motivation for all his community involvement."

"I still don't see your point".

"Bill Gordon's talked to a lot of people. He's put a lot of pieces of the jig-saw puzzle together. In your election campaign here last month, which candidate was the most vocal in his opposition to bringing new industries into town?"

"Well, except for Jim Stevens and some of the old council members, yes, that would be Fred" agreed the Chief. "But that doesn't make him a murderer".

"Isn't it also true that he got into some pretty loud arguments with one of the leading advocates of the project—Dick Barrett? Isn't it true that he accused Barrett of being interested in the project for personal gain through sales of more real estate?"

The door opened and Sergeant Gordon came in and sat down. He looked tired. The other two looked at him, waiting for him to speak.

"I think I've got what you want" he said. "Neilson left his plant at four o'clock that afternoon. He got into Eversleigh just after five o'clock, and I have a witness who saw him go into Barrett's office at five past five".

"You have a witness?" snapped Perkins.

"Yes. A Mrs Jessie Jenkins. She evidently sings in the same choir with Neilson." The sergeant went on to describe his encounter with Mrs. Jenkins.

* * * * * * * * *

Mrs. Jenkins stopped Sergeant Gordon on Main Street and said, "Officer, I have some information about Mr. Barrett's murder. I don't want to talk about it on the street. I live just round the corner. Would you come to my house?" The sergeant went with her, and as they sat in her small tidy front room she told her story.

"I came out of the Post Office that day just after five o'clock. I know it was after five o'clock, because I talked to Debbie Thornton in the Post Office. She's the secretary in the real estate office, you know. She always closes up the office right at five o'clock and takes the mail over to the Post Office. Anyway, when I came out I saw Mr. Neilson going into the real estate office."

"Are you sure it was Mr. Neilson?"

"Oh yes. I know him well. We both sing in the choir at the United Church. I couldn't mistake him."

"Are you sure this happened on Tuesday?"

"Quite sure, sergeant."

"Mrs Jenkins, why did you not report this information sooner? We've been asking for witnesses for the last three days"

Mrs Jenkins looked uncomfortable. She became hesitant. "Well, you see, I know that it was Mr. Neilson I saw. But he's such a nice man. I knew there must be some other explanation. I was sure that he couldn't be the murderer and I didn't want to get him into trouble."

"So why are you telling me all this now?"

"Well, you see, last night I saw him again at a church meeting and my conscience began to bother me. I knew I should have responded to your appeal for witnesses".

"Thank you, Mrs Jenkins. I'll make arrangements for you to sign a statement about what you've told me."

The sergeant went over to the real estate office where Debbie Thornton confirmed that on Tuesday evening she had left the office exactly at five, and that Barrett was working in his private office at that time. She went straight over to the Post Office with the mail and she confirms that she talked with Mrs Jenkins there.

* * * * * * * * * *

"That settles it" said Perkins. "Do we have enough evidence to convince you now, Carl?"

"It doesn't look too good for him, I'll admit" said the local Chief. "But I still can't bring myself to believe he's the murderer. Are you going to arrest him?"

"Just look at what we've got" said Perkins. "It was his gun. He was seen going into the office at the right time. He was fanatically opposed to something that Barrett was working for—something that he felt might jeopardize his kid's future. And if he's innocent, why didn't he come forward and tell us why he went into that office?"

"I know" said the Chief. "It's bad about the gun. It's bad that he was on the spot. It's bad that he hasn't admitted that he was there. But your idea of motive doesn't seem right to me. If that was his motive, then he has to kill all the members of that committee."

"Come on, Carl. You're not that dumb!"

Montmore blushed uncomfortably at this remark, and was about to protest. But Perkins continued, "I didn't say he went there with the purpose of killing Barrett. But he went there. We know that much. He went there an hour before Barrett's first Council meeting. Am I stretching the known facts too much if I suggest that he went there to talk about the industrial park? Maybe he thought he could change Barrett's mind. Maybe he proposed a compromise. At any rate, I suggest Barrett refused to budge an inch. We know from accounts of his campaign that Neilson had a temper when he is aroused. The shot could have been fired in the heat of temper. Now can you give me any explanation that fits the known facts more closely?"

Carl Montmore's blush had faded, though he still felt distinctly uncomfortable. "You may be right", he admitted. "But I don't like it. I just have a feeling that it can't be that way. Yes, the facts point to Neilson, and you can't ignore facts. I know that. But I still think that you're making a big jump from the known facts to the conclusion you've arrived at".

The Inspector stood up and stretched himself. If he had seemed to fill the room when he was seated, Carl felt that he had to press himself flat to the wall to allow space for the big man to stretch.

"I'm not ready to lay formal charges yet" said Perkins. "I'd like to talk with Neilson first. Bill, go over to his house and tell him we'd like to ask him some questions. Tell him we'd like him to drop over here as soon as he can. Don't put any pressure on him. If he really resists tell him there's no compulsion. We just want to get some facts straightened out. It's Saturday afternoon, so there's a good chance he'll be home".

Chapter 9.

"While we're waiting for Gordon let's you and me go get a coffee, Carl?" suggested the Inspector.

"We can have them send coffee in", offered the Chief.

"No, let's go over there. I need the exercise. And I need to get out of this telephone booth they give you for an office". Tact had never been one of the Inspector's strong points.

"Fine by me" said the Chief, feeling his anger rise again. "But let me warn you that the walls of the Hearthside have ears, and there are mouths attached to those ears".

"Good" said the Inspector. "A change of conversational topic is just as refreshing as a change of location. I assure you that I have just as many good ideas on reforming the government or managing the Maple Leafs as I have on investigating murder. Come on, let's go get that coffee".

* * * * * * * * * *

They had been back in the Chief's office for ten minutes when Bill Gordon returned. He was accompanied by Fred Neilson. The latter may have come voluntarily, but he was obviously not pleased to have been invited.

"What's all this about? Why are you trying to drag me into this business?" he demanded. He looked from Perkins to Montmore, and back to Perkins, not sure who to blame.

Both men had risen to their feet. Montmore performed the introductions. "Fred, this is Detective Inspector George

Perkins of the Ontario Provincial Police". The two men shook hands in silence as Bill Gordon went out to the general office to work on his written report. This left an empty chair for Neilson and the three of them sat down.

"Mr Neilson, I'm sorry to have to disturb you, especially on a Saturday afternoon. But, as you know, this is a murder investigation and we can't take the week-end off. Tell me, when was the last time you saw Dick Barrett?"

Neilson thought for a while before answering. "I think it would be Monday night at the Lions' Club meeting", he replied.

"You didn't see him at all on Tuesday?" asked the Inspector. Both policemen were watching him closely.

"No", he replied. "Maybe Carl hasn't told you. I work in the city. I'm gone all day. I usually get home about five thirty. I had no chance to see him Tuesday. From what I hear, he must have been dead by the time I got home".

"Did you stop anywhere on the way home on Tuesday? Anywhere at all?"

"No, I don't think so".

"What would you say" Perkins asked slowly "if I told you that we have a witness who saw you going into Barrett's office between five and five thirty on Tuesday?"

Neilson's face paled noticeably. But he gave the Inspector a steady look as he replied "I'd say that your witness was mistaken".

"Where do you keep your gun, Mr Neilson?" The Inspector's sudden change of subject seemed to surprise Neilson.

"My gun? I don't have a gun".

"I am referring to a .38 calibre revolver which was purchased in the city of Windsor six years ago and registered in your name".

"Oh, that gun!" said Neilson in a voice which suggested he had just remembered something from another life.

"I bought that when we lived in Windsor. I bought it for my wife."

"Why?"

"What do you mean, Why?"

"Why did you buy your wife a gun?"

"There had been a rash of home invasions, assault and rape cases. I was worried about Jill as I was away quite a bit on business. What's wrong with that?"

The Inspector ignored the last question and asked another of his own. "Where do you keep the gun?"

Neilson looked blank. "I really don't know. I told you, I gave it to my wife. She's never had any occasion to use it, and I'd forgotten all about it. I guess she has it stored away somewhere".

The Inspector thought about this for a minute. Then he asked, "Is your wife at home, Mr Neilson?"

"She was when I was so rudely dragged down here". Neilson was beginning to show his earlier signs of irritation.

"Oh, I'm sure Sergeant Gordon wasn't rude."

Turning to the Chief, the Inspector said, "Get Gordon back in here, will you."

Then turning back to Neilson, he said, "Mr. Neilson, I'm going to drop round and have a friendly chat with your wife. You stay here. Sergeant Gordon and the Chief will keep you company."

Neilson flushed with anger. "You can't do that. You'll scare the hell out of her. This doesn't have anything to do with her."

"Perhaps not. But that gun was discovered yesterday on the construction site beside Dick Barrett's office. One shot had been fired."

The flush of colour drained from Neilson's face. His lips moved, but no sound came. No one spoke as he tried to regain his composure.

"That's impossible!" he finally blurted out.

"Not only is it possible, Mr. Neilson. It's a proven fact. And we have the gun—your gun—your wife's gun. I want you to stay here with the Sergeant and the Chief, and while I'm gone, I want you to reconsider the answers you gave to my questions."

* * * * * * * * * *

The Inspector rang the door bell of the Neilson home. It was a well-kept home. The front garden had been tended with care. The large double windows on either side of the front door indicated it was a spacious home. The brickwork and the paint on the door and window trim was without a flaw.

The woman who answered the door was quietly attractive. Her short brown hair had obviously been styled professionally. Although she was dressed casually in a green blouse and matching pants, it was an elegant casualness.

"Yes?" She made the one word a question.

The Inspector introduced himself. "I have just been talking with your husband, Mrs. Neilson, and there are a couple of questions I'd like to ask you. May I come in?"

"Where is Fred?" she asked as she opened the door to admit him.

"He's down at the station chatting with Chief Montmore. Mrs. Neilson, I won't keep you long. I just have a few brief questions. Do you remember that about six years ago, when you lived in Windsor, your husband bought you a gun for self-protection?"

The question obviously took her by surprise. "Why, yes," she said. "But what…"

The Inspector interrupted her question, "Do you still have that gun in your possession?"

"Yes, but it's never been used."

"Tell me, where do you keep it?"

"In a small drawer in the dresser in our bedroom."

"When did you last see the gun?"

A puzzled frown crossed her face. "I really couldn't be sure. I rarely have cause to use that drawer."

"Mrs Neilson, would you please take me to that drawer and show me the gun?"

The worried frown grew deeper. "Come this way, Inspector." She led him up a thickly carpeted staircase and into the master bedroom. In keeping with the rest of the house the room was furnished with taste. She crossed the room to a low dresser and opened a small drawer. She reached in and gasped, "It's not here!"

She feverishly opened the other drawers in the dresser and tossed the contents aside without finding the gun.

She turned to face him. Her face was white. "It's gone! It's not here!"

She stepped close to him and clutched at his arms. "What's happened? What does this mean?" Her voice was rising in volume. "You knew it wasn't here, didn't you? You know where it is, don't you?"

Very quietly and deliberately he said, "Yes, Mrs. Neilson, I know where it is."

Chapter 10.

The funeral home was filled to overflowing. In addition to personal friends and mourners and all the town officials, there were the curiosity seekers and gossip mongers that are always in evidence following a violent death. Jack Porter was there and he described the service in his story for the Record:

"This was Eversleigh's version of the ceremonial funeral which Ottawa and Washington reserve for heads of state and national heroes. This was Eversleigh's tribute to a respected native son. Those who showed their confidence in Dick Barrett on election day paid their tribute to him this Monday without a dissenting vote. All members of Town Council acted as honourary pallbearers, and a eulogy was delivered by Councillor Derek Wheeler".

During the reception in the United Church hall following the service Cathy was expressing her sympathy to the grieving young widow. She knew how great a strain the ceremony must have put on Susan. "I hope you are going to be able to take some time off until you get your life back in focus," she said.

"Yes, in fact I'm hoping to go away for a while. The Inspector said it would be O.K. for me to get away for a few days to visit some friends," replied Susan. "Joe Simmons has been great. I want to keep my teaching job, but I just have to have some time. Joe's arranged for special compassionate leave for me. He's got a good supply teacher and he told me not to rush things. I have some friends that have offered to have me stay with them for a while. I guess I need to find someone who can give me a lift down to the city sometime this week."

"As a matter of fact, I'm driving down early Wednesday morning . I have an all day meeting. I can give you a ride."

"Oh Cathy, that would be wonderful! Are you sure it wouldn't be any trouble?"

"No trouble at all, Susan. How be I pick you up at your place at 7:30 Wednesday morning?"

"Great! I'll be ready," and she turned to respond to the lineup of others extending their sympathy.

Twice a year Cathy attended a regional meeting of librarians from a seven county area. This was held in the auditorium of the Central Library in the city. That Wednesday such a meeting was scheduled.

Cathy steered her red Toyota out of the apartment parking lot and drove the few blocks to the Barrett house. Susan was ready and came out of the front door as Cathy pulled into the driveway. She put her suitcase on the back seat and slid gracefully into the front passenger seat, buckling the seat belt. She turned to Cathy with a quick smile and said, "You've no idea how much this means to me. I don't know how I got through that funeral on Monday. Everyone was so kind, but the strain was just awful and now I'm at the point I just don't want to have to talk to people for a while."

They drove in silence. Cathy had so many questions she wanted to ask, but she knew she must respect Susan's desire for privacy. It was, however, Susan who was the first to break the silence.

"It's the uncertainty that gets to me," she said. "That Inspector seems sure that it was Fred Neilson. He says there's a lot of evidence pointing that way. But I don't know. I wish I could be that sure".

Susan had opened up the subject. Cathy decided to see what she got from a gently probing question. "What makes you so unsure?"

"I don't know, really. The Inspector's probably right. I guess the police usually are".

There was another silence. Again it was Susan who broke it.

"The police seem to think it was a spur-of-the-moment thing. They may be right, of course. But something had been troubling Dick for several weeks. I don't know what it was. You know, Dick never kept any secrets from me. But he just wouldn't tell me this time. He just brooded about it. I can't help thinking that his death had something to do with whatever it was that has been bothering him."

Once again there was a silence. They were approaching the outskirts of the city. Cathy was full of questions, but how could she probe deeper without upsetting Susan? For the third time Susan broke the silence.

"It started after the last meeting of that committee about the industrial park. I don't know what happened that night, but something did, and Dick was never the same."

Cathy almost ran through a red light in her excitement. She wanted to find out more about that night. And now Susan had brought the subject up. But they were almost downtown. The traffic was heavy and Cathy had to concentrate on her driving. But she must pursue this subject, traffic or no traffic.

"Did you ask him about the meeting when he came home that night?" she asked.

"No, it was too late that night. The meeting must have gone on until after midnight. I stayed up until after the eleven o'clock news, but I was asleep before he came in. It was next morning that I knew he was worried."

"But…" began Cathy. She stopped and tried to bite back the word she had already spoken. She suddenly realized the interpretation Susan might put on the words she had almost uttered.

Susan seemed not to have noticed. She was still speaking.

"In fact, late nights were becoming the rule rather than the exception. He worked late hours at the office four or five times since that meeting. And I mean very late. It never used to be like that. All I know is that he was terribly worried."

They stopped at another light.

"Cathy, I can't thank you enough for the ride. I'm sorry I've babbled on so much about myself all the way. I feel so up tight. Do you think you could drop me at the bus station?

* * * * * * * * * *

The business of the librarian's meeting kept Cathy's mind fully occupied throughout the day. Even during the lunch break she had no time to think of Eversleigh or Dick Barrett. One of the pleasant parts of these meetings was the opportunity to meet friends over lunch. Many of them were friends from college days who were now doing a similar job to Cathy in different communities across South Western Ontario. They had the same problems in common. Murder, however, was not one of those problems.

They talked about the way they expected computer technology to change the operation of libraries and about the challenge to secure adequate funding from politicians motivated by the need to cut back on expenses. So many things had changed in the few years since they had been in college, and they expected the pace of those changes to accelerate in the future.

The meeting finished at four o'clock. She had agreed to have dinner and spend the evening in the city with Joe. He said he would ride down after school with one of the teachers who lived in the city, and they had arranged to meet at five forty-five. This would allow her time to get her hair done at a place she liked and she had made an appointment for four thirty.

As she sat under the dryer her thoughts turned to Susan Barrett and the drive down this morning. One disturbing thought had been hanging in her subconsciousness all day. Now it demanded attention. It wasn't just one question, but a series of related questions. Yet they all came back to that one disturbing question. Why had Dick Barrett not got home until after midnight that night? Why had he not told Susan that the meeting adjourned at nine fifteen? Why had he been working late at the office so often in the last few weeks? Was Dick Barrett having an affair? Did Susan suspect that he was having an affair? Was she jealous? Jealous enough to murder? Was Susan Barrett really the murderer? Yes, that was the question all the others kept leading to.

Cathy told herself that was even less believable than putting Fred Neilson in the role of the killer. At least it had been Neilson's gun.

But Susan was the possessive type. "Yes," thought Cathy, "I believe she just might be capable of committing murder if she thought someone was going to take Dick away from her. But surely it would have been the other woman she'd have gone after, not Dick. Oh this is all crazy thinking!"

Joe was sitting in an uncomfortable straight-backed chair reading the evening paper when Cathy walked into the lobby of the Westminster Hotel.

"Hi, Joe. Sorry I'm late," she greeted him with a smile.

He put the paper down and jumped to his feet.

"Hello! No, you're not late. I got here a little early. I was just catching up on the news and wondering if I had time for a beer before you showed up. They've got a cosy little English style pub down the hall. Let's go get a drink."

—He took her arm and guided her towards the sign that proclaimed "The Boar's Head." Joe ordered a draft beer and Cathy agreed to try a shandy—an old English drink which is half beer and half ginger ale. As their drinks were served Cathy settled herself comfortably into her chair and crossed her legs.

"How was your day?" he asked.

"Great. The meeting was worthwhile and I always enjoy getting an update on all the gossip. By the way, I gave Susan Barrett a ride down this morning. We talked about Dick and I've got some more ideas about the murder."

"Just a minute, Cathy. Stop right there. Please! I didn't come down here to spend an evening playing detective. Let's leave all that until we're back in Eversleigh."

"I'll strike a bargain with you, Joe. Let me tell you what happened today, and explain my latest crazy idea while we have this drink. Then I promise not to bring the subject up again the rest of the evening."

"I don't want to talk about the murder at all. But if you stick to that promise I'll give you fifteen minutes to get it off your chest. OK?"

"It's a deal!" She told him all that she had learned from Susan that morning, and all the questions which had come to her under the dryer.

"I can't get Dick's late nights out of my mind," she said. "Could they possibly have anything to do with the murder or am I just letting myself get sidetracked?"

Joe ordered another round of drinks.

"I don't know about Dick's late nights," he said, "but I know Susan. She's one of my best teachers. You're not going to get me to believe that she murdered her husband. No bloody way!"

"I know how you feel. I feel the same way about Susan. But there's something funny I've got to figure out. I got started on this thing because of something Sergeant Gordon said—that detective work is a process of gathering a vast number of small details, setting them down side by side until one of them doesn't match up with the others. It's true that I don't have a vast number of facts, but I do have one fact that doesn't match up. Dick Barrett was an honest man. Everyone in Eversleigh recognizes that. Susan will tell you that. But Dick lied. That's the fact that doesn't match up. He lied to Susan. He led her to believe that the meeting had gone on until midnight. But we know it ended at nine fifteen. Where did he go during that time? Who did he spend that time with that he couldn't disclose to Susan? What happened during those three hours that upset him so much? Joe, you were there. Can you remember whether Dick said where he was going after the meeting?"

"Now you put it that way I do remember. I can answer your question. I can put your mind at rest. Then let's forget the whole thing. Two or three of us went for a coffee at the Hearthside after the meeting. I remember Dick saying he wouldn't come. He had some things he wanted to finish up at the office. When we came out of the restaurant someone said that Dick must be a devil for hard work. His car was still parked outside his office. So you see, the mystery's solved. can we now drop the subject?"

"Thanks Joe. Of course, you've only solved half the mystery. You haven't explained why he didn't tell Susan he went back to the office. But I'll keep my side of the bargain. The subject's closed for tonight".

As she drained the last of the shandy, however, she resolved to find a tactful way to have a heart-to-heart talk with Debbie Thornton as soon as possible.

They left the "Boar's Head" and walked the few blocks to Maloneys, an establishment renowned equally for the gourmet quality of its food and the calibre of its entertainment, a combination designed to make any occasion memorable. Following a sumptuous meal and an early show featuring excellent musical and comedy numbers, Joe and Cathy danced the next hour away without a thought of the murder.

As she relaxed in Joe's arms on the dance floor she found herself thinking about their relationship. They seemed to be spending more time together. Joe said he loved her. Did she love him? He sure had a way of making her feel good inside. He also made her feel that she needed him. She wanted ti be with him. "Does that mean I'm in love?" She looked up at him as they danced and their eyes met. "Yes, dammit, I think I'm in love."

They took a cab back to the lot where Cathy had parked the Toyota that morning. She took the keys from her purse and passed them over to Joe.

"You drive, Joe," she said. As he let her in on the passenger side she realized that this was the first time she had let anyone drive her car.

As they left the lights of the city behind them she eased over and laid her head contentedly on Joe's shoulder. They drove home without a word being spoken.

As Joe parked the car behind the apartment building, she said "Thanks Joe. That was a wonderful evening."

He switched off the lights, turned off the motor and gave her they keys. As soon as she had dropped the keys into her purse he turned her towards him. With one hand behind her back he pulled her firmly against his body while his other hand caressed her cheek, and then reaching behind her neck guided her face to his until their lips met. They clung to one another as his tongue pushed between her moist lips and darted back and forth in her mouth.

As they released each other he groaned, "Whoever designed this car didn't plan on its occupants getting too passionate. My body certainly wasn't meant to twist that way."

She laughed, opened the passenger door and eased herself out. Joe walked with her to the front door where they came together in another tight embrace. "Do you believe I mean it now when I say that I love you?" he asked softly.

"I'm almost persuaded!" she laughed as she pulled away from him. "Call me tomorrow, Joe".

She turned and ran up the stairs to her apartment. As she undressed she could still feel his lips pressed against hers. "Yes, dammit," she repeated, this time out loud, "I think I am falling in love."

It wasn't until she was in bed with the light out that she realized she hadn't given a thought to the murder for more than five hours.

Chapter 11.

"Try one of these cream donuts, Jill," said Nellie McLaughlin. "They're really good. I picked them up at that new donut shop that opened last week near the motel. Do you know that place is open day and night—24 hours—7 days a week! It's crazy! Who wants donuts at three in the morning? But, hey, they make good donuts!"

Nellie felt she had to keep talking in order to keep Jill Neilson's mind off the subject of her husband's arrest. But even with the help of donuts, that was an impossible task.

Jill was an attractive young woman who took care to dress well. She had her hair done regularly and never went out without taking time to apply just the right amount of make up. But not today. No amount of make up could help her tear-stained face as she sat in Nellie's kitchen.

"Nellie, be honest with me," she sobbed. "You don't think he did it, do you?"

"You know quite well I don't, dear," replied the older woman. "And when those policemen come to their senses they'll know it too."

"But they say it was my gun! It must have been my gun! It's disappeared! Who could have taken my gun?" Jill broke into another attack of sobbing.

"Jill, dear, don't torture yourself like that. They'll get at the truth soon. Here, have some coffee. And try one of these donuts."

Jill laughed through her sobs. "You're just like my mother," she said. "Whenever I had troubles as a little girl, there was always milk and a cookie to make me feel better. Now it's coffee and a donut! Alright, I'll try one, but I'm sure they must do awful things for my figure."

The two women were next door neighbours. Nellie was the wife of the town administrator. She had lived in Eversleigh all of her sixty years. She and Harry had never had a family, but she enjoyed having young people around her. When Fred and Jill Neilson had come to be their neighbours three years ago, Nellie had adopted the three Neilson children as if they were her own grandchildren. She treated Jill like a daughter and enjoyed the many chats they had over coffee in one or the other of their kitchens.

Harry McLaughlin was different. He was a man of few words. He did not show his emotions easily. He had a craggy, gruff, look about him, and the children weren't quite sure how to take him. But he did enjoy a game of euchre, and very few weeks went by without the two couples spending at least one evening round the kitchen table with the cards.

Fred and Harry had another absorbing hobby in common which they shared regularly. Chess was a game that particularly suited Harry. It could be played with few words and many long silences.

After the coffee and donuts the two women talked for an hour. When she rose to leave Jill felt better. Nellie really was good for her, she thought.

"Oh Nellie, I almost forgot the reason I came over," she said as she reached the door. "I'm driving the children down to my mother's tonight. They're going to stay there until this thing's over. They're having a hard time at school with all the kids talking. I'll have to stay down there one night before I drive back and I may stay two. Fred thinks I should, but I don't want to be away too long in case something comes up. Would you mind feeding the cat while I'm gone?"

"Of course, dear," said Nellie. "That's no problem." She put her arm around the younger woman's shoulder. "Don't worry about Tabby. We'll make sure she's fed. I'm glad you're taking the boys, and the trip will do you good too. Try not to worry too much. I know that's easier said than done. But I'm sure it will all work out right in the end."

When Harry McLaughlin came in for lunch a few minutes later Nellie told him about Jill's visit. "Have you heard any more news, Harry?" she asked.

"It's not good for Fred," was the brief response.

"You mean there's more news?"

"Got more proof," replied Harry.

There were times when Nellie was frustrated to a point of physical ache at the slow process of prying information out of her husband. For one who gave all she had so willingly when it came to information, it was simply unfair. "What kind of proof?"

"Fingerprints."

"Where?"

"On Barrett's desk."

"Oh no! Are they sure they are Fred's?"

"Carl says so."

"Harry, you know Fred couldn't have done it."

"Carl says those O.P.P. fellas are not happy with Jessie Jenkins. She was their only witness that Fred went in there. Now she's not sure. They don't think she'll hold up in court. Don't need her now. Got their own proof. Fingerprints. Want to get the case to court as soon as possible. Think it's all sewn up." This was almost certainly Harry McLaughlin's longest speech of the day.

"How do you know all this, Harry?"

"Carl. He tells me stuff. He don't like those O.P.P. fellas. Thinks they've got it wrong."

"Has Fred explained why he was in Dick's office?" asked Nellie.

"Still says he wasn't there."

"But what about the fingerprints?"

"Haven't told him about that yet. That's their trump. Looks like check mate!" Harry used his two favourite pastimes as he mixed his metaphors.

"There must be some mistake," said Nellie. Tears came to her eyes as she thought of the young woman next door.

"Fingerprints don't lie, Nellie! What's for lunch?"

Chapter 12.

About the same time that Jill Neilson succumbed to the temptation of Nellie's donut, Cathy Silcox made a decision. She picked up the phone and dialled the number of the real estate office.

"Debbie, this is Cathy Silcox. There's something I want to talk to you about. Could you have lunch with me today?"

Debbie knew Cathy, but had never been on lunch-date terms with her. She was surprised at the invitation.

"I'd love to, Cathy," she replied. "But I really can't. I only get half an hour for lunch and we're so busy over here right now. Sometimes I can ask for an extended lunch hour, but not this week."

"Then how about dropping over to my place for a while this evening," suggested Cathy.

"Sorry, I've got a date tonight."

"Listen, Debbie, it won't take half an hour. Can't you meet me at the Hearthside for lunch? It's right across the street from your office. We can eat a sandwich and talk and you can be back in time. I know it's an imposition. But I'd really appreciate it if you can."

"O.K., Cathy. But be there right at noon."

By this time Debbie was not only surprised by the request. She was quite frankly curious.

As she entered the restaurant she saw that Cathy already had a table in a booth near the back. Cathy watched her as she made her way between the tables. A slim young woman in her early twenties with blonde hair falling to her shoulders. She was wearing a smart navy blue pant suit. The wide collar of her white blouse sat neatly over the top edge of the jacket. The red nail polish matched perfectly the colour of her lip gloss. The carefully applied makeup added to the image of a professional secretary-receptionist who knew that first impressions were important in her job. However, no amount of makeup could hide the dark shadows below her eyes.

"Thanks for coming over, Debbie. Now, order what you want. They're pretty fast with service at lunch time, so we'll have lot's of time to talk and eat and get you back in the office by twelve thirty".

The waitress took their orders without delay. There was no time for preliminaries so Cathy began right away.

"We have our first regular Council meeting tomorrow. I think they're going to appoint me to the industrial park committee to replace Dick Barrett. I've got to get some background about the subject as fast as I can. Dick was pretty active on that committee. Did he keep a file in his office with his notes on the work of the committee?"

"Yes, as a matter of fact, he did."

"Do you think you could arrange for me to look at it?"

"I don't know." Debbie hesitated. "I think you'll have to get clearance from the police. They said nothing must be moved from Mr. Barrett's office."

"Oh! I didn't think about that. Debbie, how much time did Dick spend on the work of the committee? Apart from actual meetings, I mean. You see, before I commit myself to take the job I have to get some idea of what's involved."

"Well," said Debbie, "Mr Barrett was very conscientious about anything he did. Yes, he did put quite a lot of time into it. He wouldn't take time from his normal working day, so he did his committee work in the evening. I think he did a lot of studying on it at home, but the last few weeks he put in some long evenings at the office."

"Were you involved in it at all?" Cathy asked. "Or did you stick strictly to the real estate business?"

"I wasn't involved with his committee work at all until the last few weeks. He had been drawing up a report on the operating costs and the possible sources, especially the likeliehood of tax dollars being used. It was pretty detailed stuff. There were a lot of pages of figures to be typed. He did ask me to work late on those pages on three evenings. He paid me extra for my time."

"That report's something I particularly wanted to look at. Did he get it finished?"

"Yes, he finished it the week before he was killed. In fact, the last night we worked on it we stayed pretty late because he was determined to get it finished. It must have been almost midnight. He gave me a ride home that night."

They finished their lunch in silence. Debbie's eyes grew moist. She took a Kleenex from her purse and dabbed at them. "It still doesn't seem possible that all this has happened! Cathy, I just have to get back to the office now."

"Yes I know, Debbie. And thanks for telling me all this. I really appreciate it. By the way, the last report he did, the one that kept you so late, is it in the file in his office?"

"Yes it is," said Debbie. She rose to leave.

"I'll talk to the police then," said Cathy, "and see if they have any objections to my looking at it. I'll see you later."

"O.K. And thanks for the lunch, Cathy".

The conversation she had had with Debbie came back to her in bits and pieces during the afternoon while she worked. She was too busy to give it very much thought. She promised herself a good evening of study about the matter. She wondered if Susan Barrett had known that Debbie Thornton was included in those late nights at the office.

She locked the library at five thirty. As she walked towards the Post Office she noticed Ken Davey's car pull out of the alley beside the real estate office and head North. The sight reminded her that Ken was still looking for a house for her. As the car passed her she started to wave a friendly greeting, but stopped in the middle of the wave. Seated beside Ken in the front passenger seat was Debbie Thornton. The two were in deep conversation and Debbie was smiling happily.

Cathy's mind was racing. She knew that Ken and Debbie lived in different parts of the town and neither of them lived in the North end, so he wasn't just giving her a ride home. Debbie had said that she had a date tonight. Was that date with Ken Davey? Debbie seemed like a nice straightforward young woman. And Ken was a bachelor. So there was no reason they shouldn't date. And there was no reason for her to be so nosey!

But if they were serious, perhaps Ken was jealous at the thought of Dick Barrett's late nights with Debbie. Had she inadvertently discovered another suspect? "I never used to have such a suspicious nature," thought Cathy. After supper she would do some serious thinking. And she mustn't forget first thing tomorrow to call Sergeant Gordon and see if she could get permission to look at that file.

She stopped in at the grocery store to replenish her food supply. At the check out she remembered that she needed another carton of Du Maurier.

As she dropped the change into her purse, she heard a familiar voice behind her. "You really can't stay off the weed, can you?"

She turned with a smile. "Hello, Joe! How was your day?"

"Not bad. But now I've got to make the big decision as to which kind of microwaveable mush it'll be for dinner tonight. Unless, of course," he grinned, "I could convince some attractive young lady to take pity on me and invite me to share a home cooked meal!"

Without waiting for a response he headed for the frozen food section. Cathy took her two plastic grocery bags and left the store. Outside she met one of the young mothers who brought her child to the "Mother & Tot Hour" every week in the library. They chatted for a few minutes and as they parted Joe came out of the store with a grin on his face.

"I still haven't found an attractive young lady to invite me home for supper," he said.

"Did anyone tell you that reticence was not one of your strong points?" laughed Cathy. "How do grilled pork chops sound?"

"My mouth is watering at the idea. As long as you don't serve detective story for dessert!"

By this time they were walking together in the direction of the apartment building. "Come off it, Joe! Stop teasing. As a matter of fact, something else happened today, and I was planning to try and sort out my thoughts tonight. Perhaps you can help me sort fact from fantasy."

"Oh no!" he said. "If it's going to be that kind of evening I'll opt for the microwave. It was nice seeing you." He made as if to cross the street.

"Joe, don't be like that. I'm serious."

"So am I, Cathy. Deadly serious. But not about murder. I'm serious about you! I'll tell you what. I'll take you up on the pork chops and then we'll see which of us can generate the greatest interest in the other's serious pursuit!"

"You're crazy!" she laughed again. "O.K. I'll take you up on your silly game."

After supper they did the dishes together. As Cathy was putting the plates away in the cupboard above the sink she said over her shoulder, "I had lunch with Debbie Thornton today."

"Did you? And I suppose you talked about murder all through lunch. So now it's time for other things."

He put his hands firmly on her slim waist as she closed the cupboard door and spun her around to face him. Their lips met in a brief kiss. She pulled away from him.

"Debbie worked late with Dick several nights on his report for the industrial committee. He took her home about midnight one night. If Susan knew that, she would have been insanely jealous."

He let her go. "Alright. You win," he said. "Give me a beer and tell me who the suspect is tonight."

She opened a cold beer for him, curled up in her favourite chair, lit a cigarette and told him about what she had learned today.

It was late that night when he left her apartment. They had talked out all the pros and cons of the case—and Joe had left no doubt in her mind that he was very much in love with her. By the time he left she neither knew what she thought about the murder nor how to cope with the turbulent emotions that he had stirred up within her.

Chapter 13.

Cathy was not a big breakfast eater. Coffee and toast were her usual fare. As she waited for the toast to pop she turned on the radio. She did this every morning to check the correct time.

The news headlines were being read as she turned the set on. "There has been another murder in the Town of Eversleigh. More details after this message from your local bottler of Pepsi Cola."

The toast popped up. The coffee machine gurgled. The noise of the singing jingle filled the room. Cathy ignored them all. She stood motionless waiting for "more details". "Who can it be?" She said the words aloud. At this point the "who" referred, not to the murderer, but to the victim. "Damn commercials!" The jingle seemed to have no end.

"A report received within the hour from a police spokesman in Eversleigh says that there has been another murder in that town. For the past week police have been investigating the murder of a real estate agent who had just been elected mayor of the town. This morning the strangled body of his secretary was found at the bottom of a flight of steps leading to her apartment ."

"Oh God!" Cathy sat down on a hard kitchen chair. The toast and the coffee were forgotten. All she could see was the smiling happy face of Debbie Thornton in the front seat of Ken Davey's car. Last night she had been about to add Ken Davey's name to her list of suspects. But she had convinced herself that there was no foundation for such a suspicion. Now he not only had to go back on the list, he had to go to the top of that list.

As soon as she got to the library Cathy called the police station and asked for Sergeant Bill Gordon.

"This is Cathy Silcox at the library. When you were here last week, you asked me to let you know if I thought of anything that might help you. I think I have something now. Could you come over to the library?"

"Certainly, Miss Silcox," the detective said. "I'll be there as soon as I can. It may be a little while, though. Things are rather hectic down here this morning."

"Yes, I expect they are. Actually it's about Debbie Thornton's death that I think I have some information."

"Oh is it?" The detective's tone changed. "I'll be over as soon as I can".

Cathy put down the phone and walked over to the window. She stood looking out but saw nothing. Thoughts and questions chased one another around her head. How much should she tell Bill Gordon? Should she tell him that she was trying to do his job? Should she tell him about the committee meeting? About Dick Barrett's late nights with Debbie? That Susan Barrett thought the meeting didn't end until midnight?

She turned back to the desk, her mind made up. These things were not objective evidence. They were her own ideas. The fact that she had seen Debbie with Ken Davey last night was evidence. That she could not conceal. It was her duty to report it. But that was all she would report. And then she would ask for police approval to look at the file in Dick's office. After all, the contents of that file were town business. And now she was a Town Councillor.

Sally Redfern knocked on her door to announce Sergeant Gordon. He had wasted no time. Cathy rose from behind her desk to greet him. Instead of returning to her desk chair she took one of the two occasional chairs and invited her guest to take the other one.

"Miss Silcox," began the sergeant, "I gather you have some information which might assist us in our present enquiries."

"I think so," said Cathy. "It is true, isn't it, that Debbie Thornton was murdered last night?"

"Either last night or early this morning. We are still not sure of the time of death."

"Well I thought that I should tell you that I know who she was with last night. I guess I don't have the right to keep that piece of information to myself, do I?"

"Please tell me what you know."

"Well," said Cathy, "She went out with her boss, Ken Davey. You must know that she worked for Dick Barrett and Ken Davey in the real estate office."

"Yes I know that. Do you know what time they went out, when they returned or where they went?"

"No, not all that. Debbie told me yesterday at lunch that she had a date last night. She didn't tell me who with. But when I left here at five thirty, I saw her with Ken Davey. They were driving north on Main Street. I guess I assumed that Ken was her date."

"You don't know where they went, or when they got back?"

"No, that's it. It's really not very much, is it?"

"Detective work involves gathering lots of small facts. I'm glad you told me this. You said you were talking to Miss Thornton yesterday. Did she tell you anything else?"

"No. At least nothing relevant to her murder," said Cathy.

"Oh? How do you decide what is relevant and what is not?" asked the detective.

Cathy felt herself blushing. "I don't know. I mean..." She paused. His question had caught her off guard. To cover her confusion she got up and went to her desk to get a cigarette. She held the open pack towards him. "You don't smoke, do you Sergeant?"

"No, thanks."

"It helps me think." She lit a cigarette, sat back in her chair, re-crossed her legs and slowly blew a cloud of smoke to the ceiling. She had regained her composure. The detective, however, remained silent. Cathy had to say something.

"We just talked about general topics. We did talk quite a bit about Dick Barrett's work on the industrial park. Which reminds me, Sergeant, Dick had a file in his office on matters relating to that committee. I think I'm going to be asked to succeed him in that position. I asked Debbie to get the file for me. She said I would have to get police permission to remove anything from Dick's office. Can you give me that permission?" She was now in full control of herself.

"I'll talk to the Inspector about it. I doubt if there'll be any problem."

"I'd like to get it as soon as possible," she said, "so that I can do my homework on the committee. I'm not really too up-to-date on the facts."

"I'll talk to him when I get back to the office," he said. "You're sure there's nothing else you can tell me, Miss Silcox?"

"That's about it, I'm afraid."

"And you don't have any other thoughts that might help us in our investigation of Mr. Barrett's death?"

Cathy felt the blush returning. She quickly leant down to pick up the ash tray from the small table beside her chair. As she stubbed her cigarette out, she replied "No, nothing I can think of."

"Well, thank you. What you have told me was quite helpful. It confirms what Mr Davey told us himself."

Cathy was startled. "You mean he admitted he was out with her last night?"

"Oh yes. He was the first person we talked to this morning and he volunteered the information without hesitation."

"Why didn't you tell me that instead of letting me go through all this?" Cathy sounded annoyed.

"I had to find out how much you knew. You just might have told us something he hadn't disclosed."

"Did he tell you where they went?" she asked.

She started blushing again. It really wasn't any of her business where they went.

"Oh yes. He didn't make any secret of it. There was a County Real Estate Association banquet and dance in Danchester. He's an officer of the association and had to go. He's not married and he says he doesn't have a steady date. So, as it was a social occasion, he asked Miss Thornton to accompany him."

"Oh!" Cathy could think of nothing else to say. She felt deflated.

"Miss Silcox, let me ask you another question before I leave. Did you have any reason to expect that there was something more to Mr Davey's relationship with Miss Thornton? Do you know of any reason that would make you connect this murder with that of Mr Barrett?"

Cathy was beginning to wish that she had never called the detective. He asked too many questions that made her feel uncomfortable.

"No," she said. "I don't know anything beyond what I've told you".

The sergeant rose. He thanked her for her help, and left.

* * * * * * * * * * *

As he walked back to the police station Bill Gordon was reminded of the resolve he had made on his last visit to the library. He must find out more about this woman. Why would a young woman with a figure like she had want to be treated like a man? For the life of him he couldn't understand the feminist movement.

Back at the police station he found Inspector Perkins in conversation with Chief Montmore. As he entered the office the Inspector stopped talking, looked up and asked, "Did she know anything, Bill?"

"All she could tell me was that the Thornton girl had been out with Davey last night. She confirmed that they left town at five thirty. She didn't know where they had gone or when they had returned."

"That doesn't help us much," said the Inspector.

There was a short silence, broken by Bill Gordon. "Chief, what do you know about that librarian?"

"Cathy Silcox? She's a fine girl. She's got brains. She thinks. She talks well. She'll be an asset on Town Council. She's very fair minded."

"Is she honest?" asked Gordon. "Can she be trusted?"

The Chief was surprised at the question. "I've certainly never had any cause to doubt her. Why do you ask?"

"I'm really not sure. I have a feeling that she's holding something back. Oh, she answered all the questions I asked her, but I can't help feeling that she's not telling me everything she knows. And I don't quite know what to make of her. They say she's a feminist and I'm damned if I can figure out what that means. She doesn't appear to be a radical. She looks pretty— uh—feminine to me. Why would someone that attractive wanted to be treated like a man?"

The Chief laughed. "Oh, she's good looking alright. And I don't think she wants to be treated like a man. She just doesn't want people walking all over her because she's a woman. I think you've got this feminism stuff all wrong, sergeant. I wouldn't worry about Cathy."

Gordon was still uncomfortable. "I still think she knows something. She was surprised that Davey had admitted to being out with the Thornton girl last night. I think she wanted to give me the news so that I would investigate him. But she wouldn't say why."

"Well, we're certainly going to investigate him," said the Inspector. "He doesn't have any witnesses to confirm his movements after they got back to town. He says he dropped her off at her place about eleven forty five. Then he went home to bed."

Carl Montmore took up the story.

"The doctor estimates the time of death between eleven o'clock and one a.m. He can't be more precise than that."

"Which means," said the Inspector, "he could have gone round the back of the house with her, strangled her, and gone home to bed. There are no witnesses yet to support him or to convict him."

Debbie Thornton's apartment was the top floor of an old house. It was reached by a flight of outside steps against the back wall of the house.

"The doctor doesn't think the body was moved," said the Inspector, "which means that either Davey killed her when he took her home or there was someone lurking at the bottom of those steps waiting for her."

"What does this do to our case against Neilson for the other murder?" asked the sergeant. "Do you think the two deaths are connected?"

"That's what's been bothering me all morning," replied Perkins. "If it's the same murderer, that lets Neilson off the hook on Barrett's murder. He certainly couldn't have done this one. We had him locked up."

"We're going to have to make a decision pretty soon," said Montmore. We can't hold him much longer. We'll either have to charge him or let him go. With this other murder, his lawyer's going to push for a release. Debbie was Dick Barrett's secretary, and it's too much of a coincidence to think they're not connected. He'll make a strong point of that."

"I know. I know". The Inspector was irritable. "But if he's not a murderer, he's still a liar. We have proof that he was in Barrett's office that night. He still says he wasn't. He's got to be lying. And there's still the fact that it was his gun."

The Inspector stood up and stretched. Again Carl Montmore had the feeling that he was being flattened against his office wall.

"I'm going to have a talk with Neilson," said the Inspector as he left the office.

* * * * * * * * *

"Now listen to me, Neilson," the Inspector began as he sat across the table from his suspect. "My job is to get at the truth. Something's happened this morning to make some folk think I should release you. But I can't do that while you lie to me. I know you were in Barrett's office that night. I have absolute proof of that. When you say you weren't there, you just make yourself a liar. Now if you didn't kill Barrett—and there's still a question in my mind about that—but if you didn't kill him, then you're going to have to come clean and tell me why you were in his office. Keep telling your present story and you've convicted yourself for sure. What about it?"

Fred Neilson sat in silence. The Inspector could see he was fighting a battle within himself.

Finally, he sat forward and said, "Yes, I was there. I was there for about ten minutes. I talked with him. And he was alive and well when I left him."

"What time was that?" asked Perkins. "Be as exact as you can."

"As close as I can say, it was just after five. I knew his office closed at five o'clock and I had driven faster than usual from the city because I wanted to see him. I looked at my watch as I came into town and it was exactly five o'clock. He was in his office but his secretary had gone. So it must have been three or four minutes after five. I was home by five fifteen. That's three or four minutes drive from Barrett's office."

"Why didn't you tell us this before?"

"Put yourself in my place, Inspector," said Neilson. "When I heard about the murder that night the word was that it must have happened between five and five thirty. I knew I had been with him part of that time, but how could I prove that he was alive when I left him? Even now, how can I prove that? I panicked. I decided it would be better not to say anything. It was bad enough then, but when you said it was my gun that killed him I knew I must have been framed. If I admitted being there I was doomed."

"Why did you go to see Barrett?"

"It was an idea I had about this damned industrial park. You must have heard that I have been strongly opposed to the idea all along. I tried to get on Council where I could have had some say in the matter, but I didn't make it. Then I had another idea. I talked to Jack Porter at the Record. I asked him if he would run a special edition on the subject. I asked him if he would print a whole page of arguments in favour of the project facing another page of contrary arguments. I believe that I could make a strong case and that this format would help me to win support. I knew Barrett was a supporter of the project, but I knew he was basically a fair-minded man. Jack Porter had agreed and I wanted to put my idea to Barrett as soon as possible to see if he would present the case on the other page."

"What happened?" asked the Inspector.

"He agreed without hesitation. He said he would talk to Porter about it. He suggested that we start planning our pages right away. We talked for a few minutes. I wished him well at the inaugural meeting of Council. Then I left and drove home. He was still alive. And that's the truth, Inspector."

After Perkins had telephoned Jack Porter and confirmed that Neilson had at least made such a proposal to him, he went back to talk to Neilson.

"I'm going to make arrangements to release you. But I'm going to ask you not to leave town for a few days. I can't make you comply with that, of course, and I know that you work in the city, but if I kept you in custody you wouldn't be able to go to work. I'll probably want to talk to you again as we try to get to the bottom of this thing. You realize that you are still a suspect."

"No problem. I'll stay home for a few days."

"Good! I'll set things in motion to get you released."

Chapter 14.

The first regular Council meeting did not last long. Very little was achieved. The Council members were not alone in their inability to get down to work. There had been a feeling of suspense hanging over the whole town since the news of Debbie Thornton's murder. This second death had a greater capacity to produce a general state of shock than the killing of Dick Barrett. It was a cumulative effect. No one doubted that there was some connection between the death of Dick Barrett and the death of his secretary. But there was still no apparent reason for either death. And the connecting link between the two was a mystery. The questions now in every mind and on many lips were these, "Why were they killed?"

"Who will be next?"

The only empty chair at the Council meeting was that of the mayor. Dick Barrett had never occupied it. He had, however, been elected to it. It's very emptiness was a stark reminder of the facts which no one could forget.

The first item of business was to appoint a replacement for the dead man.

"I suggest we appoint one of you three who have previous council experience." said Derek Wheeler. There was a general murmur of agreement, so he continued, "George, you had the highest number of votes last week. Would you agree to take on the mayor's position?"

"No thanks," replied George Mitchell. "I really don't have the time devote to all the extra work involved. I'd like to propose Tom Hillman."

"Well," said Tom, "I appreciate your confidence, but you know I just squeaked in to the last seat by a very few votes."

"That's true, Tom, but you've been on Council longer than anyone else, haven't you?"

"Yes, I've had twelve years here."

"I'd like to second George's proposal that Tom be our mayor," said Cathy. "You'll accept the job, won't you, Tom?"

"I will if you all want me to," replied Tom, to which there was a general chorus of "We do!"

"Was that a formal motion by Mitchell, seconded by Silcox?" asked the administrator who wanted to make sure that there was an official record of the appointment.

The decision was made and Tom Hillman was ushered up to the mayor's chair and handed the gavel.

"I suppose," he began, "we now have to appoint someone to fill the Council seat that I have just vacated. Any nominations?"

The legislation gave Council the freedom to appoint any qualified citizen. Tradition dictated that they appoint the first runner-up. In this case that would be Fred Neilson who had received only twelve votes less than Tom Hillman in last week's election. There was general agreement that he should be appointed to fill the vacancy, but several councillors raised the question as to whether he was still a suspect in the murder case, and whether that should be taken into account. It was finally agreed without a vote to defer the filling of the vacant seat until the next Council meeting.

The next decision was the selection of a person to fill Barrett's vacancy on the industrial park committee. This appointment generated more discussion. Derek Wheeler had already asked Cathy to consider this position and now he formally proposed her to fill the vacancy. Other names were suggested. Although the appointment was made by Council the appointee need not be a councillor. As someone pointed out, Dick Barrett had not been a Councillor when he was appointed to the committee.

It was obvious that some members thought the appointee should have more business experience than Cathy although no one dared to suggest that it wasn't a job for a woman. She was asked what she knew about the issue.

"Well first and foremost I believe we need to attract new industry to this town And an area set aside and designated for that purpose seems to be the first step. But then there are questions about the construction of generic buildings and about what kind of incentives the town can give to attract businesses to establish here. How much can we afford out of our current tax revenue as an investment that might or might not pay off in the future?. These are the issues facing the committee now.

"What's your personal position on those questions, Cathy?" asked Bert Menzies. The other former Councillor who had been re-elected. "I don't remember hearing you take a stand one way or another during the campaign."

"That's a fair question," replied Cathy. "Quite frankly I don't know where I stand at the moment." she went on. "I've read some of the committee minutes and I'm planning to get Dick's file on the project. I understand that he did a lot of work on some aspects of the proposal and had compiled a pretty detailed report. It's evidently in his office and I've asked the police for permission to look at it. To be honest, my mind's still open about the best way to meet these costs. If you want to appoint someone with their mind made up, then look for someone else. All I can offer you is the promise that I will study every idea that is presented. I'll weigh the effects of the pros as carefully as the cons. My final vote will be a result of what I learn. Incidentally, that will be my approach to most matters that come before Council. I believe that if I come to deal with an issue with my mind made up, then there's no point in debate."

"I like that approach," said Menzies. "I"m happy to move that we appoint Miss Silcox".

"I'd be glad to second that motion," said Derek Wheeler. Although a newcomer to Council, Wheeler had been an active member of the committee and his support carried weight. Cathy's appointment was confirmed. After a few brief items of business had been routinely dealt with the meeting adjourned early.

As they were leaving the Council Chamber, Harry McLaughlin came up to Cathy. "Miss Silcox," he began, "Are you familiar with the tax implications of spending town money on projects that are not traditionally town issues?"

"Harry, would you please call me Cathy?" she said. "You call all the male Councillors by their first name. I don't want to be treated any differently."

Harry opened his mouth to say something, but changed his mind.

"No, Harry," she went on, "I don't know all the implications. I have studied the minutes of the last meeting which dealt with that subject. But I'll admit that I don't understand it all. I think that's what Dick Barrett's file is about. I hope I can learn more from that."

"I've been working with taxes all my life," said Harry. "There's not much I don't know. Come and see me one day. I'll try explain some things to you".

"Why, thanks Harry. I'll do that one day soon. I'll give you a call and find out when it's convenient."

"Any time's convenient," said Harry.

"Great, Harry. I'll be in to pick your brains."

By this time the others had gone next door to the Hearthside for their usual coffee and chit-chat. Cathy wanted to go straight home. There was a lot of thinking to catch up on. But she knew that if she didn't join the other Councillors in the restaurant they'd think she was stand-offish.

She found them discussing the murders. What else was there to talk about? She didn't say much, but she listened. Maybe she could learn something. But she was disappointed: the conversation just went round in circles getting nowhere.

Pleading tiredness, she excused herself and walked home with her thoughts. She had set herself the task of solving a murder. She had made no progress towards this goal and now she had two murders on her hands!

She chose the kitchen table rather than her usual big chair. There were things she wanted to set down on paper. She took a clean sheet of plain bond paper and started to make a list of possible suspects.

Fred Neilson must still be included, even though it didn't seem possible that he could have killed Debbie. She added the names of Susan Barrett and Ken Davey. She couldn't think of any more. She then prepared a table of significant factors, including motive, opportunity and alibi. When she had finished her table she lit a cigarette and studied the results of her work.

When considering the motive for Dick Barret's murder, she had listed "Opposition to the new industrial park" against Fred's name, while "Jealousy" was the only motive she could attribute to Susan and Ken. Fred had the opportunity to commit the murder and had no alibi. For both Ken and Susan she was forced to insert a question mark in both the Opportunity and Alibi columns.

Turning to Debbie Thornton's murder, she could think of no motive for either Fred or Ken, with "Jealousy" being a possible motive for Susan. Ken had the opportunity in this case; Fred had no opportunity, and for Susan a question mark would have to suffice. Fred had the perfect alibi while Ken had none, and again a question mark would have to be placed against Susan's name.

She decided that her next move must be to eliminate as many of the question marks in the table as possible. There were far too many of them. She would start tomorrow with Ken Davey.

* * * * * * * * * * *

She called Ken from the library next morning. The phone rang several times. Cathy was reminded that he now had no secretary. The phone was answered by a man with a quiver in his voice. She had difficulty recognizing the voice as Ken's.

"Ken, it's Cathy Silcox. Do you have time for a chat sometime today?"

"I don't know, Cathy," he replied, still in that unnatural voice. Then suddenly, sounding more like himself, he said, "Yes, I'd like to talk to you. I've got to talk to someone. Let me call you back in an hour." She could hear voices in the background.

"Ken, is something wrong?"

"I'll tell you about it later, Cathy. The police are here. We had a break-in last night." He hung up the phone.

Cathy sat still. She looked at the silent receiver in her hand. She had a premonition. More than an hour went by before Ken called back and confirmed the accuracy of her premonition. Dick Barrett's file on the medical clinic was missing.

Chapter 15.

Ken Davey had said he would drop over to the library during the afternoon. He had some matters of business to take care of first which would keep him busy until after lunch. Cathy was grateful for the delay as it would give her a chance to catch up on some of her own work. Being an amateur detective was taking too much of her time. Not for the first time since this business began, she thought how grateful she was for the quiet competence of Sally Redfern. Her work was accurate and efficient and she had an excellent rapport with the library patrons. There were many matters, however, that only Cathy could handle. There were new book lists to study. Reviews had to be read, selections made and books ordered. There was a lot of planning to be done to prepare for the new audio visual section of the library. She just had to concentrate more on her job, she told herself.

She had selected six or seven new books to be ordered and had successfully put all thoughts of the murders from her mind when there was a knock on the door. "Sergeant Gordon is here to see you," said Sally.

"Oh, tell him to come in," Cathy replied. So much for good intentions!

"Sorry to trouble you again, Miss Silcox," said the detective as he entered the office. "I seem to be taking you from your work quite a lot these days."

"That's OK, Sergeant. I know you've got a job to do. I'm only too glad to help you in any way I can. Have a seat." She moved over to the other occasional chair.

"Well," he began a little hesitantly, "it's because I don't think that you've been as co-operative as you profess that I'm back so soon."

Cathy had just placed a cigarette between her lips. At the detective's words the hand which held the lighter stopped half way. She stared at him through the flame. He was not smiling.

"What do you mean?" she asked after her hand had regained its mobility and the cigarette was safely lit.

"When I was here yesterday I had the distinct impression that you knew more about the relationship between Davey and Miss Thornton than you were prepared to admit. You were surprised that he had so readily admitted to being out with her. You wanted to give me that information so that I would investigate him. What is it that you know, Miss Silcox? What did you expect me to find out that you didn't want to tell me?"

Cathy was uncomfortable. This detective was no fool, she thought. But what could she tell him?

"No," she said. "You're wrong. I don't know anything that I haven't told you." She said the words too forcefully.

Bill Gordon appeared not to notice. He said, "You told me yesterday that Miss Thornton hadn't told you anything that was relevant to her murder. I asked you how you decided what was relevant and what was not. You didn't answer that question then. Can you answer it now?"

`Damn the man!' thought Cathy. `If I'm not careful he's going to suspect that I'm the murderer!' Aloud she said, "I don't think I can answer your question, Sergeant."

The detective did not pursue the matter. Instead he said, "Yesterday you told me that Miss Thornton had given you information about a certain file in Mr. Barrett's office. You asked me to obtain permission for you to take possession of that file. What was the real reason you wanted it?"

Cathy was horrified at the turn the conversation was taking. The austere unsmiling face of the detective did nothing to reassure her. She tried once more to stall him. "I told you yesterday that I expected to be appointed to replace Dick Barrett on the committee studying the proposed industrial park. As a matter of fact, Council did appoint me last night. I need to be aware of all the facts that Dick had gathered on the subject."

The sergeant's face did not soften. "I said the real reason, Miss Silcox."

"Are you calling me a liar?" she asked.

He did not answer her question. Instead he said, "I don't know how badly you wanted that file. All I know is that someone wanted it badly enough to break into Barrett's office last night to get it. Now, what can you tell me about that?"

"I can tell you that I didn't break into that office," she said. "And I can tell you that I don't know who did. But you probably won't believe me."

"It's not a matter of whether I believe you, Miss Silcox. It's a matter of whether you are prepared to give sworn testimony in court that you know nothing more about that file than you have told me. And that you know nothing more about the relationship between Mr. Davey and Miss Thornton than you have told me. Withholding evidence is a serious matter."

"You're trying to scare me, aren't you? Will you answer this question for me, Sergeant? Is evidence in court confined to facts, or can it include ideas and thoughts in a person's mind?"

"I think you know the answer to that," he said. He was beginning to show signs of anger. "Evidence must be confined to known facts. And it's the facts I'm asking for."

Cathy walked slowly over to her desk and with her back to him lit another cigarette even though she'd just stubbed one out. She turned around and held the pack out to Gordon without a word.

"No thanks," he said. "I don't smoke".

"Oh that's right! I remember, you told me that yesterday."

Instead of returning to her chair she perched herself on the corner of her desk, her legs swinging a few inches clear of the floor. She leaned forward towards the detective and said, "Don't you have any vices?"

"I suppose I do." he said. "I've never sat down and catalogued them".

"Well, I know my vices, Sergeant. One is that I smoke too much and maybe one day I'll do something about it. But lying is not one of my vices. And neither is breaking and entering. One of my biggest vices, I suppose, is curiosity. Legend says that curiosity killed the cat, and before it gets me killed I think I'd better tell you something."

She went back to her chair and sat down. "I guess there's quite a bit that I should tell you. Will you let me tell it without interrupting me?"

"Go ahead," he said, "but I may take some notes while you talk."

"Like most folk in town, I've been wondering who murdered Dick Barrett. The first day you came to see me, you gave me your definition of detective work. You said it was a matter of gathering lots of seemingly irrelevant details and scrutinizing them until you find one that doesn't match. That intrigued me, and I decided I would have a go at that."

"You'd have a go at what?" asked the Sergeant.

"You said you wouldn't interrupt. I'd have a go at being a detective. You see I already know a lot of the details of life in this town. I know everybody. Most folk come into the library at some point, and during the election campaign I got to know people even better. I got to know Dick Barrett. I got to respect him. I have a gut feeling that his murder was connected with his election. It wasn't a coincidence that he was killed just before his first Council meeting. I'm on that Council now. And I want to know who killed him and why. And I intend to find out."

"But…" began the Sergeant.

She put up her hand, palm flat towards Gordon. "You promised! So, I have talked to some people. I've talked to Susan Barrett and Ken Davey and Debbie Thornton. And I'm sure that Dick's murder had something to do with the industrial park, and the fact that file has been stolen suggests that I'm right."

She described her curiosity about what happened at the last committee meeting, and the change in Dick Barrett since that meeting, noticed by more than one person.

"So you see, Sergeant," she concluded, "I really was telling you the truth. I have told you the real hard facts that I know. All the rest was surmise either on my part or on the part of the people I spoke to. So it wasn't evidence, was it?"

Gordon had made notes while she talked. He closed his notebook and said, "Young lady, now you listen to me. You were right when you said that curiosity killed the cat. And let me tell you that curiosity has been responsible for the death of as many humans as cats. I advise you to stop fooling around trying to play detective before you get hurt. Police work is a skilled profession. It's also a dangerous profession. It's not a hobby for amateurs."

"O come now, Sergeant, you can't stop me thinking. You can't stop me wondering what happened, or asking questions. I bet you most of the people in Eversleigh are doing the same thing."

"Maybe I can't stop you," he said grimly. "But someone else can. It's quite probable that Miss Thornton is dead now because she asked one question too many. I don't want another murder to solve in this case."

"I appreciate the warning," she said. "I'll remember it. But you know, I haven't had any success dealing with my cigarette smoking. I doubt if I can control my curiosity any more successfully."

She got down from the desk and went back to the chair. She lit another cigarette as if to emphasize her point. She felt better for her confession. She smiled at the detective with a twinkle in her eye.

"Tell me this," she said. "Do you believe me now?"

He did not return her smile. He said, ""I assure you, Miss Silcox, this is not a laughing matter. Nor is it something to be taken lightly. Yes. I think I believe you. But that doesn't mean I'm happy. And the Inspector's not going to be happy either." He got up to leave. At the door he turned around. "If you turn up any more evidence, or get any more bright ideas, let me know."

"Evidence, certainly. I wouldn't dream of concealing evidence. But bright ideas? I'm sure you'd soon get bored or frustrated if I shared all my bright ideas with you!"

The sergeant snorted, went out and banged the door shut behind him.

Chapter 16.

Cathy managed to accomplish a fair amount of her library work before Ken Davey arrived at three thirty. She even ignored her own lunch break, although she filled in for Sally on the check-out desk while she went for lunch.

Ken was in a very agitated state when he arrived. She was not surprised at this. After all, in the space of a week his partner had been murdered—his secretary had been murdered—and his office had been broken into. But there was evidently something else on his mind.

"Cathy, I just discovered something that I don't understand. I've got to tell you. I don't know whether I should take it to the police or not. You told me the other day that you had some ideas about Dick's murder. Maybe you can explain this."

"Alright Ken, I'll try. But calm down, man. What is it?"

"Well, I was up at Jackson's farm this afternoon, doing an appraisal. He wants to sell it. On the way back I thought of something I'd forgotten to ask him. I stopped the car and got out my notebook to scribble a reminder to myself. If I don't write things down when I think of them I forget them. Anyway, when I was putting the notebook back into my pocket I dropped my pencil and it rolled under the passenger seat. As I felt under the seat for it I found this scrap of paper. Debbie must have dropped it on Tuesday night."

He handed her a crumpled piece of paper. Cathy smoothed it out and read it—'Debbie. I must talk to you privately as soon as possible. Please call me at home.' It was signed 'Susan Barrett.'

"What do you make of it?" he asked. "What does it mean? What should we do with it?"

"Not so fast, Ken," she said. "We've got to think about this. First of all, is it really Susan's writing? Would you recognize her writing if you saw it?"

"I think so. I've seen things she's written a few times. This looks like her writing, although I'm not sure I could swear to it."

"The other thing that's important is to know when the note was written. Particularly whether it was written before or after Dick's death. There's no date on it, and we don't know how long Debbie had been carrying it around."

"Yeah," he said. "That could make a difference, I suppose."

"Then again," said Cathy, "We don't know the reason Susan wanted to talk to Debbie. It might be something that had a bearing either on Dick's death, or on Debbie's. But it might have been something totally irrelevant to the murders."

"I doubt that," said Ken. "If it was something trivial she would just have called Debbie at the office. There would have been no need for a note like this."

"The trouble is that these murders overshadow everything else right now. We want to interpret everything as if it has some bearing on the murders."

"Well what do we do with the note?" he asked. "Do I take it to the police? Do I destroy it and forget about it? Do I..."

Cathy interrupted him. "Leave the note with me, Ken. I've been giving a lot of thought to the murders. I've got some ideas. Sergeant Gordon knows what I'm doing even though he's not very happy with me. But let me study this note. I have to talk to Susan about something else. I'll see if I can find out anything about the note from her. I think it has to go to the police, so if you like I'll pass it on to Sergeant Gordon. But let me talk to Susan first."

Ken seemed relieved. He rose to go, but Cathy motioned him to sit down again. "Just a minute, Ken. Remember, I called you this morning? I wanted to talk to you. All we've talked about so far is the note you found. Now can we spend a few minutes on the stuff I wanted to discuss with you?"

"Oh sure. I'm sorry. This other thing put your call right out of my mind. What did you want to talk about? If it's the house, I just haven't come up with anything suitable yet."

"No, it's not the house. I'm in no rush about the house," she said. "It's the murders I want to discuss. Ken, are you prepared to be frank with me?"

He looked surprised by her question. "Yes, certainly. Why wouldn't I?"

"Perhaps because you don't know what I'm going to ask you," she said. "For example, how well did you know Debbie Thornton?"

It wasn't a question he expected. But it didn't seem to trouble him. "Oh, pretty well," he said. "She's been our secretary since she left school. She was the only one in the office and she grew into the job. She did all our correspondence, took messages, typed up agreements and leases, and handled all the books. She was damned competent."

"That's not what I meant," said Cathy. "I was referring to your personal knowledge of her on a social level. Did you see much of her outside office hours?"

This time he looked even more surprised by the question. The tone of his answer showed that he was also annoyed by it. "You're getting rather personal, aren't you? If you must know, I didn't see her outside office hours. She was an employee, not a social acquaintance. I've always believed that it's good business practice to keep the two things separate."

"And yet you took her to a dance on Tuesday night?"

His annoyance turned now to anger. "Just what are you getting at?" he demanded.

She realized that she had been too blunt, another of her faults that she should try to rectify. "I'm sorry, Ken. I didn't mean to insinuate anything. It's this damned murder business. I just want to find out what really happened. I have a feeling that Debbie knew why Dick was murdered—maybe even who murdered him. I think that may be why she was killed. I just wondered how much you knew about her."

"Alright, Cathy. I'm sorry I flared up. I seem to be so edgy these days."

"That's not surprising," said Cathy.

"And by the way," he said, "that affair on Tuesday night was a Real Estate Association banquet in Danchester. I'm quite active in the Association and I had to be there. They had a dance afterwards and everyone was encouraged to bring a partner, so I asked Debbie. They were all real estate people. It was a social affair in a way, I suppose. But I looked on it as a business responsibility. That's why I invited Debbie. It's the one and only time we've been together outside office hours."

Cathy thought that he was being rather more defensive than was necessary. She wondered how far she dare go without him losing his temper with her again. She said, "I guess Dick didn't make the same distinction as you between employer/employee relationships and social acquaintances."

"What do you mean by that?"

She could see the temper returning. "I understand that Dick and Debbie spent some pretty late hours working together on matters other than real estate business. He was seen to take her home after eleven o'clock on at least one occasion."

Cathy was trying to see if she could detect a sign of jealousy in the dead man's partner. She thought she had been successful when he retorted, "That wasn't a social occasion. They were working on that damned industrial park. But I told him it wasn't right to keep her there alone at night. In fact, I had several arguments with him about that."

"Ken, I'm sorry," she said. "I shouldn't have pried into these things. I didn't mean to impute any wrong motives either to you or to Dick or to Debbie. Let's change the subject." He readily agreed to that suggestion.

"There is one more thing I want to ask you about," she said. "On the day Dick was murdered, was there anybody he was expecting to see who hadn't arrived by closing time? Someone who might have arrived later, after you and Debbie had left?"

"I don't know," he replied. "I left early that day—about four thirty. I went up to see Jackson at the farm. You know, the place I was at today. But he wasn't there. I went on up to a little restaurant I often eat at up the highway. It's a quaint little place run by two old sisters. It's an antique store as well as a restaurant. You've probably seen the place. It's about twenty miles out of town. It's called the Lamplighter. All I know is that Dick told me that he was going to stay on at the office until it was time for the Council meeting. Debbie left at her usual time. So anyone could have gone in without either of us knowing. The police say Neilson did. Maybe someone else did. But I don't know of anyone who had an appointment to see Dick."

"Thanks, Ken. I'm sorry I haven't been too tactful this afternoon. As you say, I think we're all a bit edgy. If I do find out anything about that note of Susan's I'll let you know."

Again he rose to leave. This time she let him go. She opened her purse and took out the table of suspects she had prepared. She thought the conversation with Ken had helped her to eliminate two of the question marks.

Chapter 17.

As she opened the door of her apartment she heard the phone ringing. She ran to pick up the receiver before the caller hung up. "Cathy Silcox speaking," she panted.

"And how's the great detective today? Solved any murders recently?"

She recognized the teasing voice of Joe Simmons and realized she hadn't seen him for two days.

"Don't tease, Joe. I really don't know whether I'm getting anywhere or not. Sometimes I think I see a pattern, but then it's all muddied up by some new facts! And Debbie's murder has really changed the whole scene."

"I know," he said. "That's what I'm worried about. I can't get the thought out of my mind that she might have been killed because she found out too many facts. And I don't want you to be the next victim. Don't you think you'd better call it quits?"

She laughed. "Have you been talking to Sergeant Gordon?" she asked.

"No. Why would I?"

"Because he said the same thing to me today," she replied.

"Which simply proves that we both know what we're talking about. Please, Cathy, call the whole thing off. Leave it to the police."

When she didn't answer he continued, "Can we get together this evening and talk the whole thing out?"

"No Joe," she said a little hesitantly, "I'd like to go over and talk to Susan Barrett this evening. How about tomorrow?"

"I don't think Susan's back in town yet. At least I haven't heard from her."

"I think she might be, Joe. She only planned to be away for a few days. I'll try her anyway. If she's not home, I'll call you back. But how about we go out for dinner tomorrow night? There's a little place up the highway that's always intrigued me. It's part restaurant and part antique store. The Lamplighter."

"I know the place. O.K. You've got a deal. I'll pick you up at the library at five thirty tomorrow." Cathy felt only a mild twinge of conscience as she told Joe that the Lamplighter had always intrigued her!

Susan Barrett answered Cathy's call a few minutes later. "Hello, Susan. This is Cathy Silcox. I was wondering if you'd got back to town yet. How did you find things in the city?"

"It was good, Cathy. My friends were wonderful. They have young children which helped to take my mind off things. And everyone was so good to me. I'm glad I went. And I did appreciate you giving me a lift on Wednesday. Actually I just got back into town late this afternoon. There are so many things to be dealt with. I had to get back."

"If you just got back, you probably don't want company yet," said Cathy. "But sometime soon I'd like to have a chat with you."

"I wish you'd come over tonight, Cathy," Susan said. "The house feels so empty. I'd love to have someone to talk to. Please come!"

"O.K. If you're sure it's not too much. I'll be over about seven thirty."

Although it wasn't too far to walk, Cathy drove over. She parked the Mustang in the driveway and rang the bell. Susan was dressed in a long casual hostess gown. As she led Cathy into the living room she offered her a drink.

"If you have any Coke, that would be fine," said Cathy. "Nothing stronger."

"Ice in it?"

"Please. You don't mind if I make myself comfortable, do you? I have a habit of slipping my shoes off and tucking my feet under me on a chair."

"That's fine. Just make yourself at home," said Susan as she brought in two large Cokes and set one on a small table beside Cathy's chair. "Would you like anything to munch on?"

"No thanks. I just ate dinner before I came out. This is a lovely room, Susan, and I love the cheerful blaze. There's nothing like a wood fire!"

"Yes, I lit it as soon as I got home. Dick always loved to sit by the fire on a winter evening."

Susan sat in the rocking chair. Cathy curled into her favourite position and looked in her purse for her cigarettes. "Do you mind if I smoke?"

"No, go right ahead!" She got up and passed Debbie an ash tray. "I used to smoke myself, but I quit about three years ago. I know that some former smokers don't like other people to smoke near them, but it doesn't bother me. Honestly!"

As Cathy lit her cigarette, Susan went on, "I was just horrified to hear what happened to Debbie. The papers and TV made a big thing of it in the city. They suggested that she must have been killed by the same person who shot Dick. If that's so, then I guess it couldn't have been Fred Neilson."

"That's right," said Cathy. "I think the police see it the same way. They've released Fred".

After a longish pause she asked, "Did you go out much while you were in the city?"

"We went shopping a couple of afternoons."

She laughed, "You know the old saying—'When the going gets tough, the tough go shopping!' But we stayed home in the evenings. These friends of mine are crazy about family board games. We played some global war game the first night. And on Thursday they had a couple of neighbours over and we all played Monopoly. That kept us up until after midnight!"

`That,' thought Cathy, `should take care of another couple of question marks.'

"Are you going back to school soon?" she asked.

"Yes, I think so. I'll call Joe tomorrow. I think I'll go back next week. I can get a few loose ends tied up over the weekend. If I stay home any longer I'll just sit around here and brood. I'll be far better off with some work to do. Anyway, I really enjoy teaching. It's quite a challenge to make history come alive for my students. To me history is so vital. It's life! Every one of us is what we are and where we are today because of history. The story of past years helps us to understand so much that is happening in today's world. But if you get me off on my favourite hobby horse, you'll never get me stopped!"

Cathy understood this. She was the same once she started talking about the role of libraries. But somehow she had to get Susan back on the subject she really wanted to discuss.

"Susan," she asked, "Does it bother you to talk about Dick?"

"No, not too much. Is there something particular on your mind?"

"Well," Cathy began, "Council has appointed me to take Dick's place on the industrial park committee. On the way to the city Wednesday morning you said that Dick had been terribly worried recently. You thought it had something to do with the last meeting of the committee. You don't have any idea what it was, do you? You see, if I'm going to take his place, I'd like to know what I'm up against."

"No," said Susan. "I don't know what it was. All I know is that there was something wrong. Dick spent hours at the office in the evenings working on the problem. I gather that he thought there was something crooked going on."

"Did he actually tell you that?"

"No. He didn't tell me anything."

It seemed as if she was going to leave it at that. She was rocking the chair at a faster rate. Then she said, "That girl of his told me!"

It was not difficult to catch the distinct note of bitterness in her voice as she spoke the last words.

"Girl?" asked Cathy as innocently as she could manage.

"Oh I know you're not supposed to use the word "girl" about grown up women these days. But I've known her since she was in High School. I even taught her! You know who I'm talking about. His secretary, Debbie Thornton. He had her in the office helping him until all hours of the night."

The bitterness was now obvious.

"Debbie told you there was something crooked going on in that committee? When did she tell you this?"

"A couple of days before he was killed. I was concerned about his moodiness. It just wasn't like him. He was so withdrawn. He wouldn't tell me anything. I was upset by all those late nights at the office. He had always shared everything with me before. There had been no secrets. Then I discovered Debbie was there typing his notes. I guess that got me more upset to think that he could share problems with her that he wouldn't share with me."

She rocked in silence for a while. Then she said, "That sounds all wrong. It sounds as though I was suspicious that they were having an affair. It wasn't like that at all, Cathy. Dick never gave me any cause to doubt his faithfulness to me. It was just that he must have explained to her what was bothering him. After all, she was typing up his report on the problem.

But he still couldn't tell me. Then I thought that she might tell me what was bothering him. So I sent her a note and asked her to call me. She called, but she wouldn't give me any details. She did say that Dick thought that he had discovered something crooked and he was trying to document it. She said I shouldn't worry about it as he expected to be finished his report in one more evening. Then she said, `I think there'll be a big explosion when he lets the cat out of the bag, and then it'll be over'".

Again Susan rocked in silence. This time the silence grew longer. Finally, Cathy broke it. "Did you talk to Dick about it after that?" she asked.

"No," Susan replied. "The afternoon he was killed I was down the Main Street shopping. I knew he was going to stay in the office until the Council meeting. I thought of stopping in to talk to him about it. But then I thought I might get him upset just before the inaugural meeting. I decided that wouldn't be fair to him, so I came straight home."

"Have you told this to the police, Susan? I mean about him discovering something crooked?"

"No. I told Inspector Perkins about Dick being worried. I told him it had something to do with the medical clinic. I didn't mention the bit about discovering something crooked. I didn't really know that, you see. It was just something that Debbie had said. There's not another person I've told about it. But when I heard about Debbie's murder I remembered it. Then today I heard about the break in at the office. It all ties in with what she told me. But I still don't understand it."

Cathy decided she had learned more than she had hoped for. She steered the conversation gently away from the subject. They talked some more about Susan's philosophy of history. They discussed the changing role of libraries. They exchanged thoughts on the amount of will power needed to break a bad habit—like smoking. Cathy knew that she didn't really mean it when she told herself she must give up the habit.

It was getting late when Cathy untucked her feet and felt for her shoes. Susan insisted on making coffee before her guest left, which provided the background for another half hour of general conversation.

"Thanks for coming, Cathy. I've really enjoyed the evening. I feel much better for it. We really must do this again," said Susan as she saw Cathy to the door.

As soon as Cathy got home she got out her table of suspects. She read it over and filled in some of the question marks. The chart now showed that in the case of Dick's death, Susan had the opportunity and had no alibi, whereas in the case of Debbie's death she had no opportunity and had a perfect alibi.

She carefully studied the changes she had made. If, as seemed likely, the two murders were committed by the same person, then it could not have been Fred Neilson. Although he had all the opportunity and no alibi on the occasion of Dick's murder, he was in police custody when Debbie was strangled. And Susan Barrett could not be the murderer. It was true that she had said she was on Main Street at or near the time of her husband's murder. Probably no one would have noticed her going into his office. She therefore had no alibi on that occasion. But at the time of Debbie's murder she was playing Monopoly with friends sixty miles away.

There were still some question marks to be filled in against Ken Davey's name. That she would deal with tomorrow evening. Of course, it was possible that the murders had been committed by different people. But assuming this not to be so, then the murderer had to be Ken Davey—or of course, some still unknown person not on her list of suspects. That was a disturbing thought on which to end the day. It would mean beginning again right at the beginning.

She had no sooner climbed into bed than a startling thought came to her. She sat up and put the light on. Was Susan's city alibi so watertight after all? Perhaps the trip to the city was part of a plan to create an alibi. Cathy had dropped her at the bus station. She had not seen any of her friends. Susan had not revealed the name of the friends. Perhaps they didn't exist. Perhaps the Monopoly game was created for the occasion. Perhaps Susan was back in Eversleigh late Tuesday night. Dick's late evenings with Debbie may not have been quite so innocent. Susan may have discovered this. There was nothing in the facts as Cathy knew them to demolish this theory. She could have slipped into her husband's office, shot him and gone home. Then that Monopoly game became important. Somehow she had to establish whether it was fact or fiction.

Chapter 18.

Sally knocked on the door of Cathy's office and stuck her head in without waiting for a reply.

"Sergeant Gordon's here, and he has another gentleman with him," she said.

"Ask them to come in. Oh, and Sally, would you bring in another chair."

She stood up to greet the two men.

"Miss Silcox," began Sergeant Gordon, "I'd like you to meet my Inspector, George Perkins."

"Good morning, Inspector," she said, shaking his hand. "Your sergeant and I have become good friends already. Please sit down," she added as Sally brought in another chair.

"I got your message, Miss Silcox," began the sergeant. He didn't return her smile and he didn't look as though he appreciated her comment about them being good friends. "The Inspector thought it was time he met you."

"I understand that you have some evidence for us." The Inspector did not waste time in chit chat.

"That's right, Inspector. I feel good and pure this morning. Just like an upright godfearing citizen should feel in the presence of two police officers."

She was smiling at them. The sergeant had an uncomfortable feeling that she might be laughing at them. The inspector didn't notice her smile.

"I promised your sergeant that I wouldn't withhold any evidence. I always keep my word."

She handed the inspector the note that Ken Davey had found in his car. He read it. He looked at her and raised his eyebrows in a silent question.

"That's my evidence. It was found under the front seat of Ken Davey's car. He thinks it must have fallen out of Debbie's purse the night he took her to the real estate banquet."

"Is this all?" asked Perkins.

Cathy's smile was now without a doubt a laugh.

"That's all the evidence, Inspector. The rest is a mixture of hearsay, ideas and suspicions which grew in my mind. You don't want to hear them, do you?"

"Now listen to me, young lady. This is a serious business. This is police business. From what I've been hearing, you've been meddling too much in matters that don't concern you. Now I want you to listen to me. I want you to stop it."

He glared at her. "But first, I think you'd better tell me what you've been up to."

"I will," she said. "I'm sorry! I was teasing you! Let me assure you that I really do know how serious this is. I'm not really as flippant as you seem to be think. I guess your official attitude brings out the worst in me. Please accept my apology. Now, I'll tell you what I've been up to, as you put it."

She told him of her visit to Susan Barrett. She told him about Debbie's suggestion that Dick had discovered something crooked going on. She told him of her thoughts about Susan in the role of the murderer and the possibility that her alibi in the city might not be valid.

"You must agree, Inspector, that none of this is really evidence. It's all surmise and is probably no more than the suspicions of an evil mind. If you think I'm crazy, forget about it. If you think it's worth checking out, I'm sure you have the means to discover whether or not Susan was in the city that night. Even the note may be meaningless. That's up to you to decide. But at least I haven't kept anything from you."

"That much I appreciate. Now will you leave the whole affair alone? Just stop snooping around. Stop asking all these questions. That's what we're trained to do. We have the means to get to the bottom of it, you know. Just trust us to do our job."

"Inspector, let me repeat what I told Sergeant Gordon yesterday. I promise that I will turn over to you any evidence I discover. But I'm not going to kid you. I can't stop thinking. I can't stop questioning. I can't stop wondering what really happened. And I'm quite sure that there are a lot of other folk in town doing the same thing. This doesn't mean we don't trust the police. It's just a very natural curiosity."

The Inspector stood up. Gordon quickly followed his lead.

"In future I suggest you keep your thoughts to yourself and keep out of this investigation. Good morning, Miss Silcox." He was already at the door with Sergeant Gordon right behind him.

Cathy concentrated on her work for the next few hours. At four o'clock she said, "Sally, I'm going down to the Town Hall. I want to get Harry McLaughlin to teach me something about computing property taxes. I'll be back before five o'clock."

She found Harry in his office working on his computer. The screen was filled with columns of figures and Harry was adding more figures to the mix. The office was fairly bare and utilitarian. Apart from the desk with the computer there were a couple of filing cabinets, a well-filled bookcase and three wooden upright chairs. Harry invited Cathy to sit on one of the chairs, which she found to be very uncomfortable; certainly not the kind of chair that would allow her to tuck her feet up under her body. There were no ash trays in sight, so she decided to forego the cigarette she would have liked to light.

"You look pretty comfortable with that computer, Harry. It must make your job a lot easier than the old way."

"That's true. I couldn't live without it now, although I did everything by hand for years. So what can I do for you today?"

"I need to know something about computing taxes and setting budgets," she said. "If I'm going to make any sensible decisions on this Council, it seems that's one of the first things I have to understand. I know we can't do much to improve the town without spending money. I know that must affect people's taxes. But just how all this works I don't know. And I think I should. Can you explain it in three easy lessons?"

"Too bad the others don't think that way," said Harry. "They think money grows on trees, they do. Do this. Fix this. Build a new road. But don't raise taxes.' "

With his economy of words he explained how the decisions of Council are translated into costs to make up the expense side of the budget. He then explained how the mill rate formula is applied to the total assessment roll. This determined how many ʻmills' of taxes would be required to provide the necessary money to meet these expenses. This mill rate is then applied to individual properties to determine the taxes each owner has to pay.

"Then Council has to go back and cut out the frills," Harry said. "Find they can't make a silk purse out of a sow's ear."

"I think I get the general idea," said Cathy. "Let's call that ʻeasy lesson number one'. Some other time you can explain to me in more detail just how you use this ʻmill rate' formula—how you know just how much tax money you're going to have available for us to spend."

"You won't have to go into all that. You won't need a lot of detail on income," said Harry. "That's accountant's work. We do that work in the office here. Council just decides how they're going to spend it."

"I know that," said Cathy. "It's just that I've got a naturally curious mind. I like to know how things work. I was the kind of kid that took alarm clocks to pieces just to see what made them go. My Dad always said I should have been a boy." She laughed. "But then he'd never heard of the women's movement!"

Harry just grunted. He had one thing in common with Bill Gordon—he didn't understand women either.

"Then for `easy lesson number three' you can tell me how all this applies to things like the industrial park. But right now I must run. Thanks for your help, Harry. See you next week."

"Bye," said Harry. He was already back at his keyboard.

Chapter 19.

Cathy got back to the library a little after five. She was locking the front door at five thirty when Joe arrived.

"I'll be with you in two minutes, Joe. Come in and sit down. Good night, Sally!", she called as her assistant let herself out. She picked up her purse from her office and went to the Ladies Room to freshen up and apply her make up. She used little or no make up during the day, but for a dinner date such as this she applied a light touch of eye shadow and outlined her lips softly with a cherry red lipstick. She checked the results in the mirror and smiled at her reflection as she anticipated the evening which lay ahead.

As they drove north on Main Street Cathy glanced at her watch. It was twenty minutes to six. As Joe swung the Olds into the Lamplighter parking lot she noted that it was on the dot of six o'clock.

As they went through the old oak doors they found themselves in the antique store. All around them were brasses, cooking utensils, lamps and a variety of other items dating back to the days of the pioneers of the County.

The elderly lady who appeared silently in the doorway at the back of the room seemed perfectly suited to her merchandise. She wore a long black dress with white frills at the neck and cuffs, and a white lace-edged apron.

"Can I help you?" she asked. The tremble in her voice matched her appearance perfectly.

"I understand you have a restaurant. A friend of ours recommended it to us," said Cathy.

"Yes, indeed. Come right through here, my dears," said the old lady. They followed her into a delightfully furnished old dining room. One wall consisted of lattice windows giving a view of a small garden. Although it was the middle of winter and there were no flowers in bloom, it was easy to see that someone took great pride in tending this garden.

From the moment they walked through the oak door they had the sensation of having stepped back into history. Cathy thought that Susan Barrett would like this place. The old lady brought them a menu that was hand-written.

"Who's your friend?" she asked. "The one who recommended our restaurant?"

"He's a real estate man in Eversleigh, Ken Davey."

Cathy sensed the tightening of Joe's muscles, but didn't dare look at him. The old lady's face lit up with a smile. "Oh yes," she said. "Ken's one of our favourite customers. He comes out regularly. Marion!" The last word was directed toward the kitchen with a sudden and unexpected increase in volume.

At the sight of the second old lady, Cathy had difficulty restraining a laugh. She had seen twin sisters in elementary school dressed exactly alike so that it was hard to tell them apart. This was the first time she had seen the same thing with seventy year old twins.

"Marion, these people are friends of Ken Davey. What are your names?", she asked as she turned back to the table.

"I'm Cathy Silcox and this is Joe Simmons." Cathy had the feeling that they were being checked over to see if they were worthy of acceptance into the family circle. Evidently they gained approval. Marion said, "We're always glad to see any friend of Ken's, aren't we Bessie?"

As she looked around the small dining room and saw that they were the only customers, the thought occurred to Cathy that the old ladies must be glad to see any prospective diner. When the two sisters retired to the kitchen Joe turned angrily to Cathy in a fierce stage whisper, "What kind of game are you playing with me? I thought you wanted to have dinner with me. But you obviously planned this whole thing as part of your detective stunt. I've had enough of this."

He was far angrier than Cathy had bargained for. In a low intense voice she tried to reassure him. "Joe, I swear I really wanted to be with you. I simply want to check one thing with the old ladies while we're here. I'm sorry if you don't think I played fair with you by not telling you that before we came. But Ken said it was a great place for dinner so I thought we could kill two birds with one stone. Please, Joe, don't be mad at me."

Further conversation on the subject was halted by Bessie's return. Joe's good humour was considerably restored by the fact that the dinner was the tastiest meal he had eaten for many weeks. The home-cooked flavour matched the hand-written menu

"That was certainly a lovely meal," Cathy said. "I must thank Ken for his recommendation. Does he come here often?"

"Two or three times a month. He's about the only one of our regular customers that comes all year round. We don't get much business in the winter. But we make up for it in the summer. This is the popular route for tourists heading for the lake."

"Ken was here last week as a matter of fact," said Marion who had come back in from the kitchen and was standing beside her twin. "It was the day of that dreadful murder in Eversleigh. That was Ken's business partner that was shot, wasn't it?"

"Yes," said Cathy. "That's right. And this week his secretary was killed too."

"That's who we thought it must be," said Bessie.

"That's terrible," said her sister. "To think, that poor man must have been killed while Ken was up here having dinner."

"What time did Ken get here that evening?" asked Cathy.

Joe coughed loudly, but Cathy didn't dare look at him. She wondered how accurate the old ladies would be in their estimate of time.

"It's funny you should ask that," said Bessie. "Because when he arrived we had a conversation about him being later than usual. It was just after six."

"Yes," her twin took up the story. "He usually comes straight from his office. He's often said that he likes to eat early. That way he has the whole evening before him."

"It was like tonight," Bessie took over the conversation again. "We had no customers. It's often like that in the winter months. Usually if we have no one by six o'clock we close up and have our own supper. We'd just decided to lock the front door when Ken arrived."

"Did he seem upset about anything?" asked Cathy.

"He did that," said Marion. "He didn't talk much that night. He did say business was bad. He said he was trying to sell a farm, but he'd had no luck. We tried to cheer him up. Told him we were low on customers too, but it always picks up in the spring. But he didn't want to talk much. Sometimes he would sit and talk a long while after his meal. But not last week."

"How is he?" asked Bessie.

"Those murders must have upset him," said Marion.

"Yes, I'm sure they have," responded Cathy. "I think it'll take him a while to get over it all."

"He's such a nice young man," said Bessie.

Joe finally got a word in to change the subject. He told them what a delightful place they had, thanked them for the meal, and paid the bill.

"We'll be back to see you again before too long," Cathy said. "I think you've gained another couple of regular customers."

They walked to the car in silence. Joe started the motor and let it idle.

"What now?" he asked.

"What would you like to do?" she responded.

"It doesn't seem to matter what I'd like to do, does it?" He still sounded disgruntled, if not angry. "I thought we were coming out for an enjoyable evening, and I discover that I've been conned into hunting for murder clues. I suppose Ken Davey's the chief suspect now?"

Cathy didn't know what to say. She was desperately torn within herself. She was so engrossed in this murder case that it was distorting her perspective. She admitted to herself that Joe had a valid complaint. She should have told him what was on her mind before she suggested coming to this place. But she felt she was beginning to get somewhere and she couldn't bear to drop it all now. On the other hand, she enjoyed Joe's company. That was an understatement, she told herself. She had come to like Joe a great deal and she didn't want their friendship to suffer.

As these thoughts raced through her mind Joe sat in silence strumming with his finger tips on the steering wheel. Cathy reached a decision. She turned and put her hand on his arm.

"Joe, I really am sorry," she said. "You're perfectly right. I should have told you why I wanted to come here. I wasn't honest with you. I wasn't fair. I had some ideas about the murder and I still do. But for now they can wait. Let's spend the rest of the evening together with no more detective talk. What would you like to do?"

She felt the tension in his arm relax. "I'm sorry I got mad," he said. "But you know I get really up tight about what you're doing. I think you're playing with fire, and I don't want you to get hurt. Won't you leave it to the police, Cathy?"

"I can't promise you that, Joe. But I'll drop the subject for tonight. What would you like to do?"

"Well, maybe we could go up to the Grand Hotel in Danchester. I'm told that they've got a good band there this week. How would you like to dance the rest of the evening away?"

She moved over to the centre of the seat and lay her head on his shoulder. "I'd love to," she said.

They stayed at the Grand until almost midnight and hardly sat out any dances. The subject of the murders was not mentioned again all evening. When they arrived back at Cathy's apartment building Joe pulled into a corner of the parking lot and switched the motor off. He turned towards her and guided her face to his.

"It's a little easier to manoeuvre in this car than in your Toyota," he muttered as they came together in a long embrace. Ten minutes later Cathy sat up. "I must get to bed," she said. "It's been a long day. Thanks again, Joe. Thanks for a wonderful evening. And thanks for being so understanding."

After she got into bed she thought back over the evening. Before she went to sleep she wanted to clarify her ideas about Ken Davey. She got out her table of suspects and studied the question marks. She began to do some figuring out loud. "He says he left the office at four thirty. He should have been at Jackson's place in fifteen minutes. Jackson wasn't home and he went on to the Lamplighter. He should have been there by five fifteen. But he didn't arrive until six! Of course he might have hung around the farm for a while waiting for Jackson."

She thought in silence for a while. Then she continued figuring aloud.

"Suppose he got to Jackson's at a quarter to five. Hung around for ten minutes or so to see if Jackson came home. Then drove back to town. He could have been back at the office between five ten and five fifteen. Neilson would have left and the chances are that no one would have noticed him going into his own office. He could have had an argument with Dick, shot him and driven to the Lamplighter. He'd have had no difficulty in arriving there by six o'clock."

She got out her pen and scratched out the question marks against Ken's opportunity and alibi. His alibi was now meaningless and he could have made the opportunity. There was one question mark left against his name. That was a motive for strangling Debbie. Certainly no one seemed to have a better opportunity for that murder. Suddenly she realized what the motive could have been. No matter who murdered Debbie, it could be that she had discovered who had shot Dick Barrett and therefore she had to be silenced. Isn't that what both Bill Gordon and Joe had been telling her in their effort to get her to stop asking questions?

It was true that she had no proof that Ken Davey was the murderer. But she could certainly show how easily he could have committed both crimes. And there was a possible motive in each case. But where did she go from here? That would have to wait for tomorrow. She put out the light and was soon asleep.

Chapter 20.

Nellie put the cards away in the cupboard. She plugged in the coffee maker. It had not been a successful game this evening. Not one of the foursome could keep their mind on euchre.

Jill Neilson got up from the table to help her neighbour make some sandwiches. Harry made no move to get the chess men. Instead the two men continued sitting at the kitchen table.

"You know, Harry," said Neilson, "I can't figure out how Jill's gun got into Barrett's office that night. Who could have got hold of that gun?"

"Someone who didn't like you," said Harry. "Someone who wanted to frame you".

"But how could anyone have got hold of the gun? Who knew that Jill even had a gun?"

"All Eversleigh knew that!" replied Harry.

"What the hell are you talking about?"

Nellie turned from the counter and glared at her husband with a red face.

"I'm telling you the truth," said Harry. "Nellie told them!"

"Harry, how can you say such a thing?" asked Jill.

"It's the truth," said Harry. "Tom Hillman told me."

"Harry! I've never talked to Tom Hillman in my life!" Nellie was furious with her husband.

"Tom's wife told him," said Harry.

"That's ridiculous! I never told Mrs. Hillman any such thing."

"She heard it at the Legion Auxiliary meeting," Harry continued to release his story in his usual tantalizing fashion. Each short sentence had to be dragged out of him.

"That's ridiculous, Harry, and you know it," said his wife, although she seemed a little less sure of herself now.

"You're not really serious about this are you?" asked Fred.

Harry nodded his head. "There was evidently a lot of gossip at one of their meetings about crime in the streets. Not just in the States. Now it's getting bad in Montreal and Toronto and even in smaller cities around here like London. Too many people have guns. My Nellie said it's not just in the big cities. She said that Jill told her so. She said that Jill's still got her gun."

Jill turned on Nellie. "Is that true? Did you really tell them that?"

Nellie didn't answer. She sat down and put her head in her hands. Through her fingers she murmured, "That meeting was more than a year ago." She sat up and glared at her husband. "And you've no right to go round repeating all that gossip!" she barked at him.

Despite the seriousness of the situation, Jill couldn't help smiling at such a charge being levelled by Nellie McLaughlin of all people. This thought broke the tension in her. She realized that nothing could be gained by the feelings that were being generated.

"I remember now," she said in a light offhand voice. "It wasn't long after we came to Eversleigh. I remember telling you how much I enjoyed town life after the city. How much more relaxed I felt. That was when I told you that Fred had bought me a gun for self-protection when we lived in Windsor and we had all those home invasions and rapes going on. Don't you remember, Nellie, you asked me if I still had the gun. And I said `Yes, but I doubt if I will ever have to use it in this town.'

I didn't make any secret about it and I didn't ask you to keep it to yourself either. You haven't done anything wrong, Nellie."

She walked across the room and put her arm around the older woman and gave her a smile. "Come on, let's get those sandwiches finished." She steered Nellie back to the counter.

"I guess you're right, Harry," said Fred. "Everyone in town probably knew we had a gun in the house. But it still doesn't explain how someone knew just where it was kept or how they got it. We haven't had any break in or anything. I know I should have kept it under lock and key. The problem is then what good is it if it's locked away when you need it in an emergency. I should have probably got rid of it anyway when we moved here. But you and I aren't going to solve this, Harry, so let's have a game of chess."

The two men went into the living room where they set up the chess board.

Jill and Nellie busied themselves with the sandwiches. They discussed the increase in food prices as well as a whole range of topics which affected their daily lives. When the chess game was over the four of them sat around the kitchen table where they did justice to the sandwiches. It was inevitable that conversation reverted to the subject that was on all their minds. Somehow they found themselves discussing possible candidates for the role of murderer.

It was Harry who said, "Davey's my choice."

"Ken Davey? Oh no! Surely not!" said Jill.

"Have it your way," said Harry. "I think you'll find I'm right, though."

"What makes you think it's him?"

"I took some papers to the site office where they're putting up the medical clinic that day. Something about more information for the building permit. I came back to the Town

Hall about five thirty and I saw Davey come out of his office. He told police he was out of town that afternoon."

"Are you sure about that, Harry?"

"I'm sure".

"Have you told the police?"

"No. I didn't realize until yesterday he'd told them he was out of town. When I saw him that day, I didn't think anything of a man leaving his own office. Except he looked sort of sick. I remember that."

"But," said Jill, "When the police asked for witnesses who might have seen someone going in or out of Barrett's office, why didn't you mention it then? Why did you let them arrest Fred?"

"I didn't think it was significant," said Harry. "I thought they were looking for outsiders. It was Davey's office too. The police talked to him the first day. I figured he'd told them the truth about his movements. Only yesterday I heard he'd said he was out of town that day."

"Well," said Jill, "You'd better tell the police now."

"Maybe I should".

"There's no 'maybe' about it. Of course you should. You know they still suspect Fred. They only let him go because they're not sure. You've got to tell them what you saw, Harry."

Fred Neilson had not spoken. He had been thinking.

"What time did you say you saw him, Harry?" he asked.

"About five thirty I got back to my office. He came out as I crossed the street".

"It has to be him, then," said Fred. "I left Dick a little before five fifteen and he was fine then. If you saw Ken leave the office at five thirty, and you say he looked sick, and he told the police he wasn't there, then it has to be him."

"That's right," said Jill. "And it was Ken that took the secretary home the night she was strangled. He must have killed them both. Harry, you must tell this to the police. I can't think why you haven't told them before now!"

"Maybe I should," said Harry again.

Chapter 21.

Saturday was always a busy day at the library. Cathy usually spent most of the day at the desk, checking books in and out, leaving Sally to restock the shelves. They usually had as many patrons on a Saturday as the other days in the week combined.

Cathy decided she must concentrate on her work today. There would be no time for playing detective. Just before noon she sent Sally to the Post Office to pick up the mail. Even though there was no house delivery on Saturday, there was often mail in the box at the Post Office. She also asked her to bring back some coffee from the Hearthside. There was something wrong with their coffee machine.

There were several people lined up at the desk to check out their books, and Cathy was processing them as fast as she could, when the telephone rang. She finished the pile of books a small girl had selected before answering the phone.

"Is that you, Cathy?" She recognized the voice as that of Ken Davey. "I think I have just the house for you. Could you slip away some time today and let me show it to you?"

"I'm sorry, Ken, it's impossible today. Saturday's are non-stop all day. I can't even discuss it with you now. I've got a line up at the counter."

"Well, can I pick you up at five thirty and show it to you then?"

She knew she wouldn't want to look at houses this evening. She was always dead tired after work on Saturdays. But he was so persistent, and she had to get back to the lineup. She agreed to his suggestion and hung up.

When Sally got back the lineup had gone and it was less hectic. She took the mail from Sally and a styrofoam cup of coffee, and headed toward her office.

"If you get a rush of people, give me a call," she said.

* * * * * * * * * * *

As she ate the sandwiches she had packed, Cathy glanced casually through the pile of mail. There was the usual assortment of official library mail—new book lists from publishers, a letter from the County Library Board, several magazines. One envelope was different from all the rest. It was the small size normally used for personal letters rather than business correspondence. It was addressed in ink using block capital letters:-

MISS SILCOX
THE LIBRARY
EVERSLEIGH

Inside was a single piece of paper. The words written on it were in the same block capitals as the envelope—REMEMBER WHAT KILLED THE CAT. That was all! She sat and stared in disbelief. Surely that damned sergeant wouldn't stoop to writing anonymous letters. Yet he was the only one with whom she'd talked about that stupid quotation. And no one could have overheard that conversation. Of that she was quite sure.

The more she thought about it, the more firmly she came to the conclusion that it had to be Sergeant Gordon. He hadn't been able to persuade her to give up what she was doing by his official request, so he was using this unorthodox approach. She was angry as she picked up the phone. When she discovered that Gordon was not in town and probably would not be back until tomorrow, her anger was mixed with frustration.

There was nothing she could do about it, however. She had to get back to work. The continuous activity throughout the afternoon drove all thought of the anonymous note from her mind.

* * * * * * * * * *

When Ken Davey arrived at five twenty five there were still several people waiting to check out their books. He sat down by the magazine table and occupied himself reading the current issue of MacLeans.

When the last person had left and Sally had locked the door, Cathy said, "We'll be a little while yet, Ken. There are several things to be tidied up and the fine money has to be counted. Why don't we leave it until tomorrow? I'm really not in the mood for looking at houses now."

"I won't rush you," he said. "Let me take you out to eat. You can unwind gradually before I show you the house."

"You don't know how to take `no' for an answer, do you?" she said. She felt irritated by his persistence. He didn't answer her. He just sat there and thumbed through a magazine. She continued with the necessary activities that had to be completed. Her irritation with him prompted her to execute her tasks more slowly and more thoroughly than she normally would have done.

She finally said "Good night!" to Sally and allowed Ken to take her to dinner. While they considered the menu she lit a cigarette. The long afternoon which she had spent at the check out desk meant that she had gone five hours without a smoke! That certainly didn't help her general mood of frustration and irritation. However, the combination of the relaxed atmosphere of the restaurant, the good food and another cigarette did much to restore her to her normal composure.

The house that Ken wanted to show her was certainly an improvement over the last one he had suggested, although it was far from her idea of a dream home. It was in a good state of repair. The size was right, and she had to confess that it was in many ways quite an attractive house. It was at the extreme north end of town. It stood in the middle of a large treed lot, set well back from the road. As she looked at the long driveway Cathy could imagine the problem she could have keeping it clear of snow. There hadn't been a lot of snow this year, but most winters were worse than this. She would have to contract with someone to plow the driveway after a heavy snowfall. The house was also somewhat isolated, with a large field on either side and an extensive wood lot behind the property.

When she mentioned the isolation, Ken laughed. "Isolation is one thing you won't have," he said. "This field is where that new industrial park will probably go."

"Oh that's right. I'd forgotten that. Well then, that settles it," she said. "Isolation is not my bag. But I certainly don't want a row of factories for neighbours. Why didn't you tell me that before?"

"Factories aren't what they used to be, Cathy. For one thing there are laws now to prevent them from creating smoke or fumes or even noise pollution. And the way they build them today they usually have more attractive landscaping than many homes."

"Still doesn't appeal to me. Come on! Let's go!"

"Just a minute," he said. They were standing in the empty hallway just inside the front door. "Before we go, there's something I've got to talk to you about. I know you are trying to be an amateur detective, but what have you got against me?"

Cathy was not prepared for this question. "What do you mean?" she asked.

"Don't play innocent, Cathy" he said. A hard unfriendly note had crept into his voice. "I know you've been snooping around checking on my movements on the night of Dick's murder. You talked to the old girls at the Lamplighter, didn't you?"

Cathy was speechless. Her mind was racing.

"Why did you do that?" he demanded.

She thought of an answer. "It was just part of my process of elimination," she said. "I've checked a lot of people's movements just to satisfy myself that they couldn't have been the murderer".

"And did your investigation prove my innocence?"

A vision of Debbie Thornton flashed before her eyes and she remembered the anonymous note 'Curiosity killed the cat'. Was it her imagination, or was there an ulterior motive in his selection of this isolated spot for this conversation?

Chapter 22.

On Sunday mornings the McLaughlins were not early risers. They had never been churchgoing people. After a late breakfast, Harry picked up the phone and dialled the home number of the local police chief. He heard it ring seven or eight times, and was about to hang up when a sleepy female voice answered. He recognized it as the Montmore's teenage daughter.

"Your Dad home?" he asked.

"I don't think so." He heard a yawn. "What time is it?"

"Little after eleven," he replied.

"They'll be at church," the girl said.

"Ask him to call Harry McLaughlin". Harry never said `please' in his life. He had decided that if he was going to talk to the police he wanted it to be the local chief. not those two Provincial fellows.

It was early afternoon when Carl Montmore returned his call. Evidently the girl was not the most efficient message taker. She had just remembered Harry's message as the family were finishing lunch.

"Something I want to talk to you about, Carl," said Harry. "In private".

"Today?" asked the chief. Although he was a conscientious policeman he was also a family man. When he had a free Sunday he liked to spend it with his wife and daughter.

"I've got to get it off my chest," said Harry. "It's about the murders"

"Why don't you come over to the house?" suggested Montmore. This way he could do his duty without deserting his family.

"I'll be right over," said Harry and hung up.

He told his wife where he was going. Although it was some distance to the Montmore house he decided to walk. He wanted to think out the best way to explain his delay in telling what he had seen.

The chief had a small den which he used as a second office at home. He invited Harry into this room and closed the door. In his usual staccato manner Harry told him what he had seen. He explained why he hadn't thought it important information at the time.

"Friday afternoon I heard something," he said. He felt uncomfortable about having to explain about this. "My office being next to yours—sometimes when the door's open I overhear things. Not listening, mind you, Carl. But sometimes it happens. Those two Provincial boys said it was a pity Davey was out of town at the time of the murder. He might have seen someone if he'd been in his office."

"I see," said the chief. "And of course you knew that he had been in the office. But you didn't want to come in and say so because you didn't want us to think you'd been eavesdropping."

"That's right." said Harry.

The two men sat in silence for a while. Carl Montmore was thinking. He was enjoying his thoughts. It seemed that fate had given him the one piece of information that might lead them to the discovery of the murderer. And if that was so he was one important step ahead of the O.P.P.! There was nothing that could please him more. While he was perfectly aware that only the Provincials had the resources and experience to work on cases of this kind, it still hurt a little that they had to come into his territory. And of course he would have to pass this information to them.

"Harry, you did right to tell me this," he said. "Leave it with me. I'll check it out. Just don't say a word to anyone about it."

As they stood up, a thought occurred to the chief. "You haven't told anyone already. Have you?"

Harry looked embarrassed. "Just my wife and the Neilsons." he said.

"The Neilsons!" The chief showed his surprise.

"Our neighbours," muttered Harry. "They come in for euchre every week. Talked about it last night."

"Oh! Well, don't tell anyone else."

Montmore realized that he had better waste no time. As soon as Harry left he called the motel where the two O.P.P. officers were staying. Inspector Perkins answered.

"I've just received some information," said the chief. "I think it's pretty important. It may give us a clue to the murderer's identity." He couldn't help a note of pride creeping into his voice.

"If it's that important, you'd better come right up here and tell us. Gordon just got back from the city. He's been following up on an alibi down there. We just opened a case of beer and we're watching the football game. Come on up, Carl."

Montmore was excited by the information he had to relay. But as he left the house he felt a twinge of conscience at the disruption to his family Sunday.

George Perkins was an avid sports fan. Hockey was his first love, but football was a close second. To him the most significant advantage of the advent of Cable T.V. was that in addition to Hockey Night in Canada every Saturday he could also watch NFL games on Sunday afternoons and Monday nights. The interruption of a football game was to him at least as sacrilegious as the loss of family time for Carl Montmore. But they were both policemen. They knew that even on Sunday afternoon duty must come first.

The chief relayed Harry's story to the two officers. He went on, "We already had Davey under suspicion for the Thornton girl's death. He was in the right place at the right time for that. But he was supposed to be out of town at the time of Barrett's murder. If this information is true—if he did leave the office at five thirty, but told us he was out of town, I think we've got something important."

"Yes," said the Inspector. "That's obvious. But if this is true, how did we miss the flaw in his alibi? You checked that out, Bill. What did you find? Run it by me again."

Bill Gordon consulted his notebook to refresh his memory.

"He told me he left the office at four thirty. The secretary confirmed that. He said he had gone to see a Mr. Jackson on a farm. This Jackson wanted to sell the farm. I checked out there. I talked to Mrs. Jackson. She said Davey was there about five o'clock. Wouldn't swear to the exact time. But it seemed to fit. She said her husband wasn't home, and that Davey waited around for a while because she expected her husband home any minute. She thinks he was there about twenty minutes, and then he said he would stop back another day. She told him she was sorry that he'd had the trip for nothing, but he said he was going in that direction anyway. He said he was going to a restaurant called the Lamplighter for supper. It's a few miles farther up the highway. I went there and confirmed that he had, in fact, been there for supper. They said they knew him. He often eats there. It seemed as though he'd been telling the truth."

The Inspector looked dubious.

"Are you quite sure of your information, Carl?" he asked.

"Yes," replied the chief. "No doubt of it. Harry McLaughlins not the kind of man to imagine things."

"Well, maybe we should check it out more carefully. Bill, you go around and talk to Davey. Try to pin him down to times. What time did he leave that farm? What time did he arrive at the restaurant? See what he tells you, and see if you can find a loophole in his alibi."

"You want me to go now?" Sergeant Gordon was also a devoted football fan.

"I think you'd better," said the Inspector. "If there's any truth in McLaughlin's story, and if he's told the Neilsons we can expect a call from Neilson any minute. If it's true it puts Neilson in the clear. And anyway, once McLaughlin starts talking it won't be long before it gets back to Davey. You'd better get to him first."

After the detective left Perkins turned the T.V. on again. "Have a beer and watch the game, Carl."

"No thanks. I've got to get back to the family. Give me a call if you get anything."

* * * * * * * * * * *

Bill Gordon found Ken Davey watching the same football game. He was surprised to see the detective on a Sunday afternoon.

"You working overtime, Sergeant?" he asked.

"Just checking a few details. Do you mind if I come in?"

After the T.V. had been turned off and they were seated, Gordon asked, "Mr. Davey, you told me that you left your office at four thirty on the day of Dick Barrett's murder, that you went out of town on business, and that you didn't return until later in the evening. We have now received information that you were back in your office before five thirty."

"The bitch!" Ken spat the two words out with a violence for which the detective was not prepared. He was also at a loss to understand the relation of this response to his statement.

Davey appeared to be more angry than defensive. "The lousy bitch!" he repeated. "I thought she believed me. I never thought she'd go running to you with my story. I guess it just goes to prove the old saying—'You can't trust a woman."

"Mr, Davey, would you mind explaining to me just what you are talking about."

"Don't try to be funny with me, Sergeant. And don't try to protect her. I know damn well that Cathy Silcox has poured out my story to you. Well, it's true! Every single word I told her is true."

Bill Gordon was still bewildered by the response he had generated. But he was beginning to see some light.

"Well, Mr. Davey, just in case Miss Silcox distorted any of the facts you told her, would you mind repeating your story to me in your own words."

"Alright", agreed Ken. "I left the office at four thirty as I told you before. I went up to see Jackson. He wasn't in. I was going on up to the Lamplighter for supper, but when I left Jackson's place I remembered a magazine article on antiques that I'd been reading. It was rather an unusual article and I wanted to discuss it with the old ladies at the Lamplighter. I decided that I would slip back to the office to get it. As Jackson wasn't home, I hadn't been at the farm as long as I expected to be. I went into the office and picked up the magazine from the top of my bookcase. Then, on my way out through the front office I thought I'd just wish Dick luck for his first Council meeting."

He stopped speaking and his eyes seemed to glaze over. After an awkward silence, the sergeant prompted him, "And?"

"I opened the door to his office—and there he was—dead! I just stood there for a minute. I couldn't believe it! I made sure that he really was dead, and then I panicked! I know that I shouldn't have done it, and I've regretted it ever since. But I was afraid that I would be suspected. How would I be able to prove my innocence? I know it was stupid. I know it was wrong. But I got out and drove up to the Lamplighter and pretended that I didn't know anything had happened. Once I'd done that, I didn't know how to tell you the truth. When no one reported seeing me back in town I decided to let sleeping dogs lie."

"Why did you decide to tell your story to Miss Silcox?" asked Gordon.

"She's being playing `amateur detective," replied Ken. "She told me that right after the murder. She must have suspected me. I don't know why. But I discovered that she'd been checking up on my movements. Yesterday I heard from the old ladies at the Lamplighter that she had been out there, and that she had particularly asked what time I got there that evening and whether I appeared to be upset. I tackled her about it last night. I told her the whole story, and I thought she believed me. Anyway, I'm glad it's all out now. The deception has been weighing on my mind."

"I'm sure it has," said the sergeant. "By the way, just to set the record straight, Miss Silcox did not say anything to us about your conversation with her. I came to see you this afternoon because another independent witness has just come forward and told us that he saw you leave your office at five thirty that day."

"Oh my God!" gasped Davey.

He took a minute to digest this information, and then asked, "What are you going to do about it?"

"My job at the moment is to gather factual information. It will be up to the Inspector to decide on any action. He may want to talk to you himself. In the meantime, is there any more information you can give me?"

"No. I've told you everything now".

"What time did you get back to the office when you went for the magazine?"

"I can't pin it down to the minute. It must have been five twenty or a little after. I wasn't in the building more than five minutes and I was driving out of town again, I remember, at five thirty. I checked the time then because I know the old ladies at the Lamplighter usually close up at six o'clock in the winter if they don't have any customers."

"Did you enter your office by the front door or the side?"

"The front. The side door goes right into Dick's office."

"When you came in, did you hear any sounds coming from Mr. Barrett's room? Did you hear, for example, the sound of anyone leaving by the side door?"

"No, Sergeant. I heard nothing at all."

* * * * * * * * * *

Back at the motel the Inspector digested the information Bill Gordon gave him. "So we now have two of them who admit to being at the scene of the murder at the appropriate time. Neilson says he left at five ten, and Barrett was alive. Davey arrived at five twenty or a little after and Barrett was dead. We have three choices—Neilson killed him and is lying: Davey killed him and is lying: or if they are both telling the truth, someone unknown to us came in and shot Barrett and left again between five ten and five twenty."

"At least," said Gordon, "we've narrowed the time to a fifteen minute period."

"That's true," said Perkins, "only if both men are telling the truth. And I'm not yet prepared to accept that premise. I think it's much more likely to be one of the two we know about."

"You may be right," said Gordon, "but we've got problems no matter which one we choose. If it's Neilson then we have to find another murderer for the girl. If it's Davey we've got no problem there. He was with her the night she died. She may have discovered that he killed Barrett and he killed her to keep her quiet. But we still have the question—how did he get Neilson's gun?"

"I think," said the Inspector, "that you had better work on the gun angle, Bill. You know, I've got a feeling that Davey's more likely to be our man than Neilson." As he went over to turn the T.V. on again he turned back to the Sergeant.

"And another thing, Bill. You'd better talk to this Silcox woman and tell her to stop meddling in this business. She could get herself hurt, you know."

Chapter 23.

At the same time that Inspector Perkins decided that Ken Davey was the most likely suspect, Cathy Silcox was reaching the same conclusion.

The realization made her shudder. She thought of that isolated house in which she had been alone with him last night when he faced her with his accusation of snooping on him. He had been violently angry. She thought he was going to strike her. Her thoughts had raced to the strangled body of Debbie Thornton.

Then he had gained control of himself and taken her out to the car. As they had sat there in the dark driveway he had told her his story, just as he had told it later to Bill Gordon. She assured him that she believed him. And in fact she had believed him. His words and his manner carried conviction.

But now she wondered if she had been too gullible. Just how does one sort out the truth from the lies?

They had driven back in silence and he had dropped her off at her apartment without getting out of the car. Although it was not late she was completely exhausted. She filled the bathtub with water as hot as she could bear it, threw in some fragrant bath salts and soaked herself for a long time in an effort to take away the ache of the tension. She was in bed and asleep by nine thirty.

Unlike the McLaughlins, Cathy was an early riser on Sundays and this Sunday was no exception. She followed her usual practice of attending the early Communion service at the Anglican Church. After the service she walked home with Derek Wheeler. He was treasurer at the Church.

"How's your detective work coming, Cathy?" he asked.

"I really don't know," said Cathy. "I'm still working at it. But there's so little to go on. Sometimes I think I'm making progress and at other times I'm not at all sure."

"Have you got any suspects in mind?" He asked the question with a smile, not expecting a serious answer.

"Yes, as a matter of fact I have three."

"Good heavens! Really! Who are they?"

"I don't think I should tell you, Derek. I don't have any proof about any of them. All I have are ideas and I'm sure I'd be laying myself open to slander or worse if I were to tell anyone."

He didn't know how seriously to take what she was saying. "Well, tell me this," he said. "Am I one of the suspects?"

She laughed. "Not at the moment. But I add a new one every day, so you'd better be careful."

He changed the subject. "You know there's a meeting of the industrial park committee tomorrow night?"

"Yes. I'm looking forward to that. I've got a lot to learn. Will there be any more discussion at tomorrow's meeting about the tax implications?"

"No, I don't think so," he said. "We accepted Harry's report at the last meeting. You saw the table he prepared showing the comparison of present and projected tax income. That will be appended to our final recommendation to Council."

"Talking about that last meeting, Derek, reminds me of something. I've been told that Dick was very upset after the meeting. Was there some argument or fight in which Dick was involved, either during the meeting or after it finished?"

"No, there was nothing like that. In fact it was a short meeting simply to receive Harry's report. Nothing to upset anybody."

"I see. Well, I guess I've got to do some more homework before I really understand all the tax implications. I had a basic lesson from Harry last week. I must get him to give me another lesson soon."

"Harry's hard to talk to at times," said Derek. "But he knows his stuff when it comes to things like taxes and municipal legislation in general."

They had reached the Wheeler house. Cathy hurried home. The walk to church on Sunday morning always made her hungry. It was the only morning in the week that she cooked herself a substantial breakfast.

As she ate the bacon and eggs she found her thoughts returning to the subject of taxes. She couldn't get it out of her mind that both Ken and Susan had pointed to the last meeting of the clinic committee as an occasion that seemed to have had a profound effect on Dick Barrett. In fact, they had both suggested that something happened that night that ultimately led to his death. But Derek Wheeler had assured her that nothing had happened. All they had talked about was taxes. Either there was something mysterious that she was missing in a simple table of taxes or else Derek wasn't telling her everything.

Now there was a possibility she hadn't considered before! She had finished eating. She poured another cup of coffee and lit a cigarette. Derek Wheeler? Was he not being frank with her? Should she add him to the suspect list? Surely not. He was one of Dick's closest friends. But that didn't rule him out, did it? And he was the one that found the body after the inaugural dinner. But that didn't rule him out either. In fact, it might have been a clever tactic for the murderer to return several hours later and find the body. There may even have been some reason he had to have the body found that night.

But why? What possible motive could Derek Wheeler have for killing Dick Barrett? None at all. Unless something funny really did happen at that meeting. She would have to talk some more to Harry McLaughlin or to some of the other members of the committee. Then she remembered that Joe was on the committee. In fact, come to think of it, Joe had told her the very same thing—that nothing had happened at that meeting to upset Dick. If that was enough motive to suspect Derek, then she had to include Joe as a suspect too, and that was absurd! Damn it, she had to talk to Joe some more about this tax thing.

The sleepy voice with which he answered her call indicated that, like other Eversleigh residents, Joe was not an early riser on Sunday. The telephone, in fact, had wakened him from a deep sleep.

"Joe, it's Cathy. Are you busy today? I'd like to talk to you. And I won't kid you this time. I want to talk about the murders. If you come over, I'll make you lunch!"

"I'm too sleepy to argue," he replied. "And lunch sounds good. Give me an hour to shave and shower and get myself organized."

After lunch he helped her with the dishes while the coffee machine bubbled through its routine. She told him about the anonymous letter and her visit to the house at the north end of town with Ken Davey. She told him the questions she had about Derek Wheeler, and that she was still curious about that meeting of the committee.

She poured the coffee and they took it into the living room. As she lit a cigarette, he said—"Now let's deal with one thing at a time. I assume that there's very little point in my wasting time telling you again to stop meddling in this affair. You're just too stubborn to listen. But at least will you use some common sense, and not go getting yourself into dangerous situations alone with potential murderers. And..."

"Just a minute, Joe. Be fair!" she interrupted. "I didn't know he was taking me to such an isolated spot. And anyway I didn't think he knew I had been checking up on him."

"You just didn't think—that's the problem," said Joe. "And that reminds me. Why are you out house hunting? Or is that just another cover-up for your detective activity? Because if you're seriously looking for a house, I have a perfectly good one."

She looked at him sharply. "What on earth are you talking about?", she asked.

"I have a very attractive house. It would not be difficult to give my upstairs tenants notice to leave. Then you and I could get married and you wouldn't need to go house hunting with Ken Davey!"

"Are you out of your mind?" she gasped. She inwardly cursed herself for the awareness of the flush that had come to her face.

Joe laughed easily. "You don't have to treat it as a definite proposal of marriage if you don't want to," he said. "But I'm serious enough about the idea that I'd like us to think about it when you've finished with these mad schemes you've got in your head. And perhaps the idea even has enough interest for you to stop you going on any more expeditions with Davey."

"I do believe you're jealous!" she teased. "But you don't have to worry. I'm not going anywhere else with him." She didn't trust herself to make any comment on his startling suggestion, so she turned the conversation back to the anonymous letter. They spent the rest of the afternoon discussing the implications of the letter and the details of the committee meeting.

It was early evening and Joe was still with her when she received a phone call from Bill Gordon.

"I've been in the city for a couple of days," said the detective. "I got back into town this afternoon and found a message that I was to call you."

"It wasn't that urgent, Sergeant. You didn't have to worry about it on a Sunday."

"Every day's the same to me," he said, "when I'm working on a case like this. Do you have more evidence for me?"

"I don't think it's evidence. I was simply going to ask you whether you wrote me a letter."

"A letter?" Bill Gordon sounded genuinely surprised.

"Yes", said Cathy. "Short and to the point. And not signed".

"Miss Silcox, you're not seriously suggesting that I sent you an anonymous letter, are you?"

"I am".

"What did this letter say?"

"Listen, Sergeant. If you wrote it, you know damned well what it says. And as you haven't yet denied writing it, I'm still waiting for an apology!"

"I wrote no letter. You ought to realize that. I think we'd better talk some more about this. I'd like to see this letter. Would it be convenient for me to come round there to see you now?"

"Certainly. Any time you like, Sergeant."

"I'll be there in a few minutes."

"That was Sergeant Gordon," she said as she hung up the phone. "He says he didn't write the letter. He's coming over."

"Now?"

"Yes. He says he'll be here in a few minutes. But you don't have to go," she said quickly as Joe got to his feet.

"No, I don't want to get mixed up in this case any more. And anyway, I have some work I have to catch up on. Thanks for lunch. And think about what I said about the house. I really meant it."

He took her face in his hands and guided it to his until their lips met. "I love you," he murmured.

Cathy threw her arms around his neck. "Joe, darling, I love you too," she sighed. "Very much!"

The ringing of the door bell brought them back to earth. Joe was zipping up his jacket as Cathy let the sergeant in.

"Sorry if I'm disturbing you, Miss Silcox," said Gordon, looking at Joe.

It was Joe who answered. "Not at all, Sergeant. I was just leaving. But I'd be grateful if you could do me a favour while you're here."

"What's that?" asked the detective.

"Convince Miss Silcox to stop playing detective!" He grinned at Cathy who opened her mouth to speak, but was cut off by the detective who said, "I've tried very hard already to do that. And I'll keep trying. I'm glad to hear that you see this matter in a sensible light, Mr. Simmons."

"Good luck!", said Joe as he pulled the door to behind him. Cathy was not sure to whom this wish was directed.

"Come in, Sergeant," she said. "Let me hang up your coat. Make yourself comfortable. At least I can offer you a little better hospitality here than at the library. Would you like a beer?"

"No thanks," he said as he settled himself into the big chair recently occupied by Joe. "I'm sorry, I forgot," Cathy laughed, "that policemen on duty can't accept a drink. Or isn't drinking one of your vices?"

"Oh, I enjoy a beer occasionally," said the sergeant, thinking of the case he had left at the motel and realizing that the Inspector would be doing full justice to it by now.

"Well, I'm going to pour myself a cold glass of Coke", said Cathy. "How about you?"

"Alright, I'll join you in a Coke," he said. "Thanks!"

Cathy brought in the glasses and set one on the table by the detective's chair.

"Now what's all this about a letter?" he asked.

Cathy gave him the letter. Then she sat in the other big chair and tucked her feet under her. While Gordon studied the brief letter she lit a cigarette. He put the letter down and examined the envelope, front and back.

"You received this yesterday?"

"Yes. Sally picked up the library mail from the post office box. This was amongst all the rest."

"What made you suggest that I might have written it?"

"The other day you and I had a conversation about that quotation. You remember that, don't you?"

"Of course I do. But..."

Cathy interrupted. "I don't think I had a similar conversation with anyone else. So my natural assumption is that you were re-emphasizing your advice to me."

"Surely, Miss Silcox, you know that police officers don't go around writing anonymous letters to people."

"I suppose it is a little out of character, when I think about it. But how else do you account for it? Who do you think wrote it?"

"I would say that it was either written by the murderer, or else someone wrote it with the hope that you would think the murderer wrote it."

"But what about the quotation?" she asked.

"That could be a coincidence. It's a well known saying." He didn't sound very convincing. Bill Gordon didn't easily believe in coincidences. "Much more likely that you used the same quotation when you were talking to someone else. Have you thought about that possibility?"

"Yes," she said. "I have. And I can't be sure."

"Well, you'd better keep thinking until you are sure," he said, "for your own sake. And when you are sure, you'd better tell me. The answer to that question might be of vital importance. Now", he continued, "while I'm here, do you have anything else you want to tell me about?"

"No, I don't think so".

"Are you quite sure?"

She had the feeling that he was beginning to get angry.

"Certainly, Sergeant. Is there something else that you think I should talk to you about?"

"I was expecting that you would tell me about your conversation with Mr. Davey." Cathy stared at him in disbelief. "You mean last night?"

"I mean the conversation in which he admitted to you that he had been in Dick Barrett's office at five thirty on the day of the murder."

Cathy was horrified! She thought furiously, trying to decide what she should say. She stalled for time as she slowly lit another cigarette.

"Sergeant Gordon," she said, "you are a most remarkably efficient detective. I don't know how you do it!"

The compliment, if that's what it was, had no effect on him.

"I would like to know," he said, "why you chose not to tell me about this conversation. You agreed that you would inform me of anything significant that you discovered. I would have thought that the knowledge that a man admitted to being at a murder scene within minutes of the crime must be considered significant."

"Sergeant, I said that I would turn over to you any evidence. This conversation was hearsay. If you already know all about the conversation, then you know that Ken said Dick was already dead when he went into the office. If I suspect him of not telling me the truth, I don't think my suspicion is evidence."

"You're begging the question, Miss Silcox. Tell me this. Do you suspect him of not telling the truth?"

"I'm honestly not sure. Last night I did believe that he was telling the truth. But on thinking it over today I don't feel so confident. I'm not sure what I think."

"Let me warn you again as seriously as I can that you're playing with fire, young lady. Will you please stop playing the fool before it's too late."

She didn't answer him. He continued, "And will you go over in your mind every conversation that you have had with Mr. Davey, and ask yourself whether or not you or he ever mentioned the cat being killed by curiosity. And if you remember such a conversation, will you call me without delay?"

She started to say something and then changed her mind.

"Perhaps you already remember such a conversation?" he asked.

"No," she said. "At least I'm not sure. I was trying to remember when you arrived. It's possible, but I'm not sure."

He stood up to leave. "I hope," he said, "that you've learnt a lesson. Now please stick to things you understand and leave the police to do their job. Good night!"

"Before you leave, Sergeant, will you tell me something. Your trip to the city, was its purpose to check what I told you about Susan Barrett?"

"There you go again!" he said.

"But was it?" she persisted. "Hey, be fair! It was me that gave you the idea."

"Alright. If it will set your mind at rest, I'll tell you that, amongst a number of other things I had to do, I was able to confirm that Mrs. Barrett was in fact playing Monopoly with her friends at the time of Miss Thornton's murder."

Chapter 24.

"Good morning, Mrs. Neilson. I'm Sergeant Gordon. I'm with the Provincial Police and I'm working on the case of Mr. Barrett's death. There are a few questions I would like to clear up. May I come in?"

"Certainly, Sergeant," said Jill Neilson. "Come right in. But I'm afraid my husband's not in at the moment. He's gone for a walk. He walks every morning now. I do hope it won't be long before you can let him go back to work."

"I don't think it will be more than a few days now, Mrs. Neilson, before we can bring our investigation to a conclusion. But it isn't your husband I wanted to talk to this morning. I'd like to ask you a few questions."

"I see. You know, I'm sure, that your Inspector was here himself, and I answered all his questions."

"I appreciate that, Mrs. Neilson. But if you wouldn't mind?"

She led him into the living room. "Please sit down, Sergeant, and tell me how I can help you."

Jill Neilson was a neat, attractive woman in her early thirties. "Not beautiful", thought Bill Gordon, "but certainly good-looking. Attractive in a low key way." She was reasonably tall, not slim but certainly not plump either. No make-up, but she didn't really need it. He had a feeling that she would be a comfortable person to live with. The room in which they sat was clean and neat, but had a lived-in feel to it. "I'm sorry to have to intrude into your life again, Mrs Neilson," he began. "But I'd like to ask you some questions about that gun. You kept it in a drawer in your bedroom, I understand?"

"Yes that's right. One of the small drawers in my dresser. I showed the Inspector when he was here."

"Yes, I'm aware of that,and if you wouldn't mind, before I leave, I'd like you to show me that drawer too. But first, can you tell me specifically when you last saw the gun?"

"The Inspector asked me the same question," she said. "I think it was several weeks ago. You see. I have never gone to that drawer specifically to check that the gun was there. I've never had to use the gun. I never expected to use it. And it was in a drawer that I very rarely use. It's a small drawer in which I keep my evening bag and some accessories that I wear with my formal gown. I only wear that gown on special occasions, and they are few and far between. I think the last time was the Warden's Banquet in Danchester."

"Was the gun in its usual place then?"

"I think so. But you know, I couldn't be one hundred per cent certain. You see, I just took out the things I needed. I didn't make a point of looking for the gun. But I think I'd have noticed if it was missing. I know that's not very helpful, Sergeant, but it's the best I can do."

"Did you keep it loaded?"

"Yes. Fred bought it for me in Windsor when there was quite a rash of assaults on women, and he was away quite a bit. He insisted that I kept it loaded or it wouldn't be any good in an emergency. Although the safety catch was always on."

"I see. You have young children, don't you?"

"Yes, three. A girl who's almost ten and two boys aged six and eight. They're staying with my mother out of town until all this is over."

"Has it never occurred to you, Mrs. Neilson, that it could be dangerous to keep a loaded gun in an unlocked drawer with young children in the house?"

Jill's face went red. "Do you know, Sergeant, that thought has never entered my mind. You must think I'm an awful parent! And I guess I am. But the children never go into our bedroom. It's not that we've made a big thing about it being off limits or anything. There's just nothing for them to go in there for. But I can see your point. But I've no intention of ever having a gun in the house again, I can assure you!"

"I hope you mean that, Mrs. Neilson. Quite apart from the danger to the children, the fact is that the laws in this Province have changed since you acquired that gun. You may not have realized it, but you were keeping an illegal weapon."

"Oh my, God! I didn't know that."

"Perhaps before I ask you any more questions, you could show me the dresser in question."

"Certainly. Come this way."

She led him up the thick carpeted staircase to the master bedroom at the back of the house. She indicated the low oak dresser which stood in the recess created by the bay window.

"This is the drawer where I kept the gun." She pulled open the top left hand drawer.

Bill Gordon examined the windows behind the dresser.

"Do you always keep these windows locked?" he asked.

"In the winter we do. Once the storms are in place we don't open them until spring."

"Have you any evidence at any time of the windows being forced? Either these or any other windows in the house?"

"No," she replied.

The sergeant studied the dresser, taking particular note of the depth of the drawer in question and its present contents. He looked around the room and opened the door which led into the en suite bathroom. They went back downstairs to the living room and sat down again.

"Do you lock the doors when you go out, Mrs. Neilson?"

"If we're going far we do. But if we're just going next door, we don't bother. I often stop over and visit with Nellie McLaughlin next door. Sometimes I'm there for an hour or two. I don't lock the door then."

"Have you ever had any indication of anyone getting into the house while you're out?" he asked.

"None at all," she answered.

"Are you in the habit of entertaining much? Do you have parties or invite folk in for the evening?"

"Sometimes we do have people in. I suppose the McLaughlins would be our most regular company, although we usually go to their house rather than them coming here. We did have a bit of a party around the end of October."

"Who were your guests at that time?"

"Well, there were the McLaughlins, of course. There was Rev. Sanders and his wife from the United Church. Fred sings in the choir there, you know. Joe Simmons, the High School principal was here. The mayor, Jim Stevens, was here with his wife, Fran. And there was Jack Porter, the newspaper editor and his wife. She's president of the women's group I belong to at the church. It was a mixed kind of group, but not a wild one. We had a nice party, though."

The detective made a note of the names of those who attended the party.

"I wonder," he said, "did you by any chance use your bedroom for your guests to set down their coats that evening?"

"Why yes, as a matter of fact we did," she said, a little surprised by the question.

"I notice that there is a bathroom opening directly off your bedroom. Did you invite your guests to make use of that bathroom when they took off their coats rather than go to one on a different level of the house?"

"How do you know all these things, Sergeant? Yes, we always use that bathroom when we have company. It's so much more convenient".

"So it would have been quite possible for any one of your guests to find themselves passing through your bedroom briefly on their own. This would have afforded them the opportunity to take your gun from the dresser drawer without being observed." Jill was horrified when she realized where the sergeant had been leading the conversation.

"But none of those people would be capable of murdering anyone. That's a horrible thought!"

"It certainly is, Mrs. Neilson. But then, murder is a horrible act. You see, we can't get away from the fact that somehow, at some time, someone took that gun from the drawer of your dresser. Assuming that it wasn't you or your husband, then it had to be either an intruder or a guest in your house. You tell me that you have seen no sign of intruders. I have simply pointed out a fairly simple method by which a guest may have gained possession of the weapon. I have not said that it was one of the guests at that particular party. Perhaps you could think back and remember any other guests you may have had in your home over the past few months."

"The thought of what you suggest makes me shudder," she said. "But I guess I have to admit that I see the possibility that your idea just could be true."

"By the way," he said, "if I may change the subject for a moment. How well do you know Ken Davey?"

"You mean Dick Barrett's partner? Oh, hardly at all. We did deal with him when we bought the house three years ago. But we don't really know him. Why do you ask?"

The detective ignored her question. He asked another one himself.

"Has Mr. Davey been to your house for any reason at all in the past few weeks?"

"Not to my knowledge. As far as I know, he's never been in the house since we closed the deal. Unless he was over to see Fred sometime when I was out. But I doubt that. Fred's never mentioned it."

"O.K. Now, could I ask you to sit down with your husband later today and write down a list of all the people that either one of you can think of that have been in your house during the past few months. Particularly those who were here for an evening and who might have used the bathroom off your bedroom. Give me a call when you've completed your list, and I'll come and pick it up."

"We'll do our best, Sergeant, but it just doesn't seem possible that one of our guests would have done such a thing."

"I just have one other question," he said, "and then I'll leave you. Can you tell me how many people knew that you had a gun?"

To his surprise the question produced a chuckle.

"Would you believe all of Eversleigh?" She told him about the conversation at the McLaughlins. Actually, Nellie McLaughlin was the only person she had told, but Nellie had evidently broadcast the information at a Legion Auxiliary meeting. So 'all of Eversleigh' may not be too much of an exaggeration.

"Thank you, Mrs. Neilson," he said. "You really have been most helpful. You won't forget that list, will you?"

As he drove away, he glanced in the rear view mirror and saw a car turning into the street from a cross street about two blocks away. As he pulled up at the next STOP sign he noticed that the other car had stopped in front of the Neilsons' house. The man who got out of the car and walked up to Neilson's front door was Ken Davey, the man who never visited that house!

"Now that," thought Bill Gordon, "is very interesting."

He continued to think about the possible purpose of Davey's visit as he drove back to the
station to make his report to the Inspector.

Chapter 25.

"What's the chance of my getting easy lesson number two today, Harry?" Cathy Silcox stuck her head through the door of the Administrator's office. Being Monday, it was Cathy's day off and she was dressed casually in an old pair of jeans and a heavy loose-fitting sweater.

Harry McLaughlin looked up from his desk. "I don't know what more I can tell you," he said.

She walked into the room and stood by the desk. "Come now, Harry. Last week you just gave me an introduction. We agreed that this week you would explain to me in more detail how you use the mill rate formula—how you know just how much tax money there will be for the year."

Harry seemed less hospitable than last week. "I told you last week," he said, "that's my problem. You're a Councillor, not the Clerk-Administrator. You do your job. I'll do mine."

"But Harry, my job will be to make decisions. I need information to make the right decisions."

"Right. We'll do the computations. We'll give you the figures. You make your decisions. Then we'll tell you how much increase or decrease that will make in the mill rate."

She decided to risk doing the wrong thing. She picked up a pile of files off a chair and carefully placed them on a corner of the desk. She sat on the chair and opened her purse.

"You don't mind if I smoke, do you?" she asked as she took out her cigarettes and lighter.

"Not particularly," he said.

She sensed that his lack of enthusiastic hospitality indicated he would rather not have her visit too prolonged. She lit a cigarette. From a desk drawer he produced an ash tray.

"Harry, a Councillor can't be a rubber stamp. If I don't know how the figures are arrived at, how do I know they're right?"

He went red in the face. "Are you saying that you don't trust me?"

She realized that she was not succeeding in building a good relationship. "I'm sorry," she said. "I didn't mean it that way. It's just that I think I was elected to be responsible. Maybe you think I'm being overly conscientious. But I think people expect their elected representatives to know what they're doing, and to be certain that the decisions they are making are based on the correct facts. I think this is especially true in fiscal matters."

Harry merely grunted.

"Believe me, Harry," she went on, "I don't want to take your job away. I don't want to do all your paper work. That's your responsibility and I trust you to do your work well. But I think I should have some knowledge of how the figures are arrived at."

"You're wasting your time," he said. "But if you must know, here's what happens. The Provincial assessor decides the value of every piece of property. These are all added up to get a total assessment roll. Then you set your tax rate."

"So far, so good. But just how do you arrive at that tax rate?"

If you have a tax rate of .008, you get taxes of $800 for every $100,000 of assessed value. If you need more money, you raise the tax rate. If you need less money, you lower the tax rate. Every point gives you $100 for every $100,000 in assessed value. Understand?"

"I'm beginning to get the idea," she said. "Now, how does all this relate to the industrial park?

"You can set different tax rates for residential, commercial and industrial properties," he explained. "You figure out the extra costs to service the area—sewers and stuff. Then you set the tax rate the same way. Got it?"

"I think so," Cathy was hesitant. "I need to go away and think about it."

"Then. If they want, Council can agree to waive the taxes for the industrial park for an initial period as an enducement. It's like giving them a grant, if you like, but you have to know how much you're giving them."

"I see," said Cathy.

"That's just the local taxes," Harry went on. "The County sets a tax rate, and there's still education taxes. You got to put them all together before you send out the tax bills."

Cathy got up. She carefully replaced the files on the chair.

"Thank you, Harry. You've been a great help. I won't take any more of your time. Will you be at the committee meeting tonight?"

"I expect to be," he said.

"Good. Then I'll see you there."

* * * * * * * * * *

She left the Town Hall and walked across the street to the real estate office. A new secretary, someone not known to Cathy, was working on the computer in the general office. The sight of this woman doing Debbie Thornton's work sent an involuntary shudder through Cathy.

"Is Mr. Davey in?" she asked.

"No. He went out for a while," she said. "May I help you?"

"No thanks," said Cathy. "I wanted to talk to Mr. Davey personally. Do you know how long he expects to be out?"

"I don't think he should be too long. He went to see Mr. Neilson. Can I get him to call you?"

"No. I'll go over to the Hearthside and have a coffee. I'll stop back in about twenty minutes and see if he's returned. By the way, my name's Cathy Silcox. Is this your first day on the job?"

"Yes. I'm Nancy Scott. We just moved to town last month. My husband works in the administration office at the hospital."

"Good to meet you, Nancy. I hope you'll enjoy Eversleigh. You can tell Ken that I dropped in to see him, and I'll be back in about twenty minutes." As she crossed the street she noticed Fred Neilson coming out of the post office. She stopped to greet him.

"Good morning, Fred! How are you?"

"Oh, good morning Cathy! I guess I'm as well as can be expected in the circumstances. How are you enjoying your new responsibilities on Council?"

"It's still early," she replied. "I haven't had a chance to get my teeth into anything yet. But I'm looking forward to it. Have you seen Ken Davey this morning?"

"No. Why? Should I have seen him?"

"I just left his office. The new secretary told me that he had gone round to see you."

"To see me? Why on earth would he want to see me? I have no business with him. Wonder what he wants."

Cathy's curiosity was now aroused. She had intended talking to Ken Davey about something quite different. But now the question uppermost in her mind was why her leading suspect wanted to talk to her number two suspect. The question was so intriguing that she almost didn't hear Neilson speaking. She was suddenly aware that he had asked her something about not working.

"Oh, Monday's my day off," she said. "At least it's supposed to be, but I don't always take it."

"Then if you're not in a hurry," he said, "may I buy you a coffee?"

She was delighted at the opportunity to talk with him. He was the one possible suspect she hadn't spoken to since the murder. They went into the restaurant and he led her to a table in the farthest corner.

"I heard the other day," he began, "that you have been doing a little detective work."

"Who told you that?" she asked.

"I'm not sure now," he said. "But once a story like that starts the rounds in Eversleigh, it's common knowledge before the day's out. Is it true?"

"Yes, it's true," said Cathy. "Not that I'm having any success. It's just that by nature I'm a very curious person. I've been asking questions to satisfy my curiosity."

"I certainly wish you luck," he said. "As you can probably imagine, there's nothing I'd like better than to see this case solved. Have you discovered anything at all? Do you have any prospective suspects picked out?"

"Yes and no," she said. She was purposely evasive.

"I'm not trying to embarrass you," he said. "Let me re-phrase that. Do you have any prospective suspects other than me?"

She laughed. "I still have to answer `yes and no," she said. "Yes, I have a list of people who might be guilty, and no I can't tell you who they are. I don't want to lay myself open for slander."

"I guess you have a point there. Are you working in co-operation with the police or strictly on your own?"

"Half and half," she said and laughed again. "I do sound evasive about everything this morning, don't I? You see, I'm co-operating with the police in the sense that I'm keeping them informed of any evidence I discover. But I think they'd rather that I kept my nose right out of it. I don't think they would agree that we are working in co-operation."

"I wonder what Davey wants with me?", said Fred. "You're quite sure that it was me that he was looking for?"

"Yes. Nancy, the new secretary, told me that he had gone round to see Mr. Neilson. That's all I know. I told her that I'd come back in twenty minutes. Why don't we both go over there now and see if he's back."

"Good idea. Let's go".

As they left the restaurant Ken Davey's car pulled into his parking space beside the office.

"There he is," said Cathy. "Now we'll solve the mystery." She took it for granted that she would be included in an explanation of the reason Ken wanted to see Fred, although she realized it may well be none of her business.

They crossed the street and reached the office as Ken slammed the car door shut. "Fred, I've been looking for you," he said in surprise. "I've just been round to your house. What brings you here?"

"Cathy told me that you wanted to see me," he replied.

"Cathy did!" Ken turned to her with a puzzled frown. "How did you know that I wanted to see him?"

She grinned at him. "I thought you knew by now that amateur detectives know everything!"

"That's not funny, Cathy. And it reminds me, I've got a bone to pick with you. But let's not stand out here in the cold. Why don't you both come into the office."

Cathy was delighted at the way things had worked out. It looked as if she was going to have her curiosity satisfied on the subject of Ken's interest in Fred. As they entered the general office Cathy looked over at the new secretary.

"Hi Nancy! I found him."

Ken turned to her. "I see you didn't take long to get to know Nancy!"

The three of them went into Ken's office. He closed the door and indicated some comfortable chairs.

"Fred, I've just been round to your house," he repeated. "I've got a feeling that the police have bumped you out of the number one suspect spot, and substituted me. I'm expecting to be arrested at any time. This sort of gives us something in common. I wonder if we could pool our knowledge somehow and help each other off the hook."

"But what makes them suspect you?" Fred asked. "I can see why they sank their teeth into me. It was my gun, sort of. I still don't understand how it got here, but somebody must have got hold of it somehow. And then they discovered that I had talked with Barrett after five o'clock. But what have they got on you?"

"Little Miss Sherlock here," said Ken in a voice heavy with sarcasm, "wanted to do her public duty. She informed the police that I came back to the office after you left."

Cathy sat bolt upright in her chair. "I did no such thing!" she spat the words at him. "At least not until you had told them the whole story yourself. Then that damned sergeant came and gave me hell for withholding information from him."

Ken opened his mouth to say something. Then he shut it again. He tried to remember his conversation with Sergeant Gordon yesterday afternoon. Neilson looked from one to the other, but he couldn't follow their argument. He was, however, deeply conscious of the things Harry Mclaughlin had said the other night.

"Now just a minute," said Ken slowly. "Yesterday afternoon Sergeant Gordon came to see me at home. He told me that he had received information that I was back in my office before five thirty on the day of the murder."

"Did he say that he received that information from me?" asked Cathy.

"I don't think he actually said that," Ken said. "But you were the only person I had told. Naturally I assumed that you were his informant."

"He came to see me during the evening," Cathy said. "He was very angry with me for not telling him of our conversation—the conversation in which you told me you were back in the office. But how did he know about that conversation?"

"I guess I told him," said Ken. "I assumed that you had already told him, so I admitted having the conversation with you. But in that case, who was his informant?"

"Obviously someone who must have seen you entering or leaving the office," she said. "But I can't think why they've waited until now to speak".

Fred Neilson had been trying to break into the conversation. He knew that Harry McLaughlin claimed to have seen Davey, but he hadn't been sure whether or not Harry was mistaken. But this was different.

"Are you admitting that you were, in fact, back in the office after I left, and before five thirty?" he asked.

"That's right," said Ken.

"Did you see Barrett?"

"Yes. I went into his office. He was dead".

Neilson had trouble catching his breath. If someone had talked with Barrett after he had left, then he was in the clear once and for all. Ken's last three words hit him like a pail of cold water.

"What time did you get back?" asked Cathy.

"About five twenty"

She turned to Neilson. "What time did you leave Barrett?"

"Ten or eleven minutes after five."

"Neither of you saw or heard anything of each other at all?" Both men shook their heads.

"Did Dick say anything to you about expecting anyone else?" she asked Neilson. "Not a thing."

"How did he seem?"

"He appeared quite normal. Nothing strange in his manner at all."

"If you are both telling the truth," she said, "then someone sure got in and killed him and got out again pretty fast. And how was it that no one heard the shot?"

"With that construction gang working outside the window, you couldn't hear a thing," said Ken. "And even if someone did hear it, they'd think it was one of those bulldozers."

The phone on his desk rang. He picked it up. His face went pale. Before he had set the receiver back in its cradle, the door opened to admit Inspector Perkins and Sergeant Gordon.

"Well, I must be leaving," said Fred Neilson as he jumped to his feet.

"Yes, I should be on my way too," said Cathy. She was not as anxious to leave as Neilson was, but she knew that the policemen would not do what they had come to do in front of her.

As they left the office Bill Gordon eyed them both with a curious look. Not for the first time in his life, he wished that he could read minds.

Chapter 26.

As Cathy opened the door of her apartment she heard the telephone ringing. She managed to reach the instrument before it stopped.

"Hello! Cathy Silcox," she said. She was out of breath.

"Miss Silcox," said a frail female voice at the other end of the line, "I heard that you are investigating Mr. Barrett's murder."

Cathy had to strain to hear the words.

"Who is that speaking?" she asked.

Her question was not answered. Instead the voice continued, "Is that true, Miss Silcox? Are you investigating the murder?"

"In an informal way, yes," she said. "The police are naturally conducting the investigation. I'm simply trying to satisfy my natural curiosity."

There she was, using that word again. She must have mentioned the cat proverb to someone.

"We're all curious, Miss Silcox. But they tell me that you're getting warm. Do you know who the murderer is yet?"

"Listen," said Cathy. "I don't know who you are. I don't know who told you that I'm investigating the murders. But for your information, no I do not know who the murderer is. Do you?" Cathy asked the question as an afterthought. She was startled by the confident reply.

"Yes, I think I do. That's what I wanted to talk to you about."

Cathy pulled a kitchen chair over to the phone and sat down. Her purse hung from her shoulder still. She was able to unzip it and reach a cigarette while still holding the receiver to her ear with the other hand. As she flicked a flame onto the lighter she heard the frail voice in her ear.

"Are you still there, Miss Silcox?"

"Yes I'm still here. You say you know who the murderer is. Are you going to tell me?"

"I don't think I should do that over the phone," said the voice. "You hear all sorts of things about people listening in to telephone conversations. Even on private lines. Do you know how they could do that, Miss Silcox?"

"No," said Cathy. "I don't. But who are you? If you tell me where you live, I'll come over there and you can tell me what you know in total privacy."

"Yes, that would be better. You know, Miss Silcox, I didn't think I would have to tell you my name. I thought you'd recognize my voice."

"It does sort of sound familiar. You're not…"

"Don't say it!" snapped the voice, losing much of its frailty. "If people can listen in, I don't think I want them to know who I am. But if you don't say my name I'll give you a clue."

"Alright," said Cathy. "Go ahead".

She was sure this absurd conversation must be all a dream.

"I'm one of your most regular customers at the library," said the voice. "And I always read detective stories. I was asking you last week whether you had any more Agatha Christie books that I hadn't read."

Cathy knew now why she hadn't recognized the voice. It was Millie Brownlee, and the frail quiver was all camouflage.

"Yes," she said, "Now I know you. Are you at home?"

"Yes. Will you come right over? If you do, you'll make sure you're not being followed, won't you?"

"Oh yes," said Cathy with a smile. "I'll take good care of that. Thanks for calling. Goodbye!"

Without a doubt old Miss Brownlee had been reading too many detective novels. Whatever it was that she had to say was probably a figment of her imagination, but she'd better humour her. Cathy had intended to make herself some lunch when she got home. However, she decided that if she delayed her visit to Millie Brownlee, the old lady would think she had been kidnapped en route. She went back downstairs, started the Toyota, and drove across town to the little stone cottage that Miss Brownlee had shared with her widowed sister until the latter's death last year.

As she parked the car the thought crossed her mind that this was just the kind of house she was looking for. It was small and manageable and it had lots of character.

Miss Brownlee had arthritis and moved slowly with the help of a cane. She took Cathy into the front room. Although all the furniture was old, it was certainly comfortable. Cathy resisted both the urge to tuck her feet up on the chair, and the desire for a cigarette. Something told her that Millie Brownlee would not approve of either of her weaknesses.

"I hope you didn't mind my disguising my voice," said Miss Brownlee. "But I know from all the detective books I've read that you have to be careful when you use the telephone. You weren't followed were you?" Her voice had now regained its usual strident quality.

"I'm sure you did the right thing, Miss Brownlee," said Cathy. "And no, I'm quite sure I wasn't followed. You say you think you know who the murderer is?"

"That's right. And as no one seems to be on his track, I thought I'd better tell you what I know. I don't like the idea of going to the police. But when I heard that you are working behind the scenes like Miss Marple in those Agatha Christie books, I thought I'd tell you."

Cathy thought she'd never get to the point. "And who is it that you suspect?" she asked.

"Its Tom Hillman," said the old lady. She sat back with the look of a magician who has successfully pulled a live rabbit from his hat. If she had in fact produced a live rabbit she would not have surprised Cathy any more!

"Tom Hillman!" she said in amazement. "But what makes you think it was Tom?"

"You make yourself comfortable, dear, and I'll tell you the whole story."

At the phrase `make yourself comfortable', Cathy caught herself in the act of kicking off her shoes. She stopped herself in time.

"The day before Mr. Barrett's murder," began Millie, "I went in to talk to him. Ever since my sister died last year my nephew's been trying to persuade me to move into the County Home for Senior Citizens. I don't want to go there, but to keep him quiet I have begun to make some enquiries. They want to know what my assets are worth and the value of any property I own. So I went to talk to Mr. Barrett about having the old place appraised. The young girl he had, you know, the one that was strangled, she told me he had someone with him. She asked me to wait. I sat in the outer office and she went into the other office to talk to the other partner, Mr. Davey. While she was gone I heard voices in Mr. Barrett's office. They were getting louder. They were arguing about something. I couldn't catch the words. Then the door opened, but no one came out right away. I heard the voices clearly now. I recognized Tom Hillman's voice. He was shouting. He sounded very angry. "If you do that, Dick," he said, "you'll mess everything up. I'm not going to let you do it. I'll find a way to stop you." Then he walked out and banged the door. He strode right out of the office and slammed the outside door too."

Cathy was following the story with interest now.

"Was Debbie Thornton still in Mr. Davey's office all this time?" she asked.

"I didn't see exactly when she came out of there. I was concentrating on the men's argument. But as soon as Tom slammed the outside door, I heard her say, "I'll ask Mr. Barrett if he'll see you now." She might have heard the words that I heard, and then she might not. I didn't actually see her come out of Mr. Davey's office."

"You say this was the day before Dick Barrett's murder?"

"That's right."

"Why haven't you told the police about this before?" asked Cathy.

"At my age I didn't want to get involved." said Millie. "And anyway, I was sure the police would get to the bottom of it without my help. And another thing. I couldn't believe that Tom Hillman could be a murderer. I've known him since he was a little boy. And his mother before him. They're a good family."

"Then why have you told me now?"

"It began to bother me that the police don't seem to be getting anywhere. But I still didn't want to get mixed up with the police. Then yesterday at church I heard that you were working in the background like Miss Marple. I thought maybe you could check it out and see if it means anything. That way my conscience would feel better."

"Thank you Miss Brownlee. I don't know that I deserve your confidence. I'm no Miss Marple. But I will follow up what you've told me. You do realize, don't you, that if there is anything in it, then I'll have to let the police know?"

"Yes dear, of course. But I'm sure you'll know best."

Cathy drove home in a state of mental confusion. Like Miss Brownlee, she found it hard to picture Tom Hillman in the role of murderer. But, if it came to that, she couldn't really believe any of her other suspects were murderers either! And certainly the incident Millie had described to her could not be ignored.

It was three o'clock when she got home and she had still eaten no lunch. She put the coffee machine on and made herself some sandwiches. The thought of Tom Hillman as the murderer had never occurred to her. She was sure it had never occurred to the police either. It was unlikely, therefore, that anyone had checked his alibi. The longer the time since the murder, the more difficult it was to check people's movements. It is usually possible for a person to remember exactly what they did for one day. But after two weeks, it's often hard to remember which day a certain thing happened. To pin it down to a time becomes unrealistic.

Cathy thought back to the day of the first murder. She remembered Joe had been at the library and he had walked with her to the Town Hall. They had met Tom Hillman outside the Town Hall. He was coming from his men's wear store further down Main Street. But that had been about quarter to six. It would have been quite possible for him to have been in the real estate office at five fifteen, and been back in his store for almost half an hour. How could she check his movements that day? He had two assistants in the store, but she could hardly walk into the store and ask them "Do you remember whether your boss was out of the store between five and five fifteen on the Wednesday before last?" On the other hand, how else could she even make a start?

Suddenly another thought occurred to her. Tom Hillman lived in that big white frame house on the street behind Debbie Thornton. She closed her eyes and tried to picture the exact location of the two houses in relation to each other. She thought they must be almost back to back. That meant that in the case of Debbie's death, Tom Hillman perhaps had as good an opportunity to be on the spot as Ken Davey. The whole case was too confusing. She had a list of suspects already made up with motives and opportunity and alibis. Now she had another name. But there was not enough evidence to build a case against any one of them.

She decided that if she was going to have the clear mind needed to participate sensibly in the meeting of the clinic committee, she had to get out for a brisk walk and clear her head of all these suspicions. She walked south with no specific destination in mind. It must have been some kind of subconscious auto-suggestion that led her to the street on which Debbie had lived. Her apartment was the top floor of an old frame house. It had been re-designed to make it completely self-contained. It could only be reached by means of a flight of steps against the back wall of the house.

Immediately next to the house was an empty lot. It had an uncared-for look, with weeds, old bricks and stubby bushes covering the uneven surface of the ground. Immediately beyond this vacant lot was the front of a big white house. Cathy was certain that this was Ton Hillman's house. There was a low fence between the Hillman house and the empty lot, and no fence between the lot and the house with the apartment.

At the hour Debbie had returned home that night there would have been no one on the street. In the darkness it would have been easy for the murderer to cross the empty lot unobserved. Cathy shook her head as if to get rid of a growing suspicion. She turned down the next side street towards Main Street. As she walked back up Main Street towards the centre of town she glanced at her watch. It was ten after five. She didn't know what to do about supper. The call from Millie Brownlee had delayed her lunch until mid-afternoon, and she wasn't hungry now. But she knew she would be starving before the meeting was over.

She had reached no solution to this problem by the time she reached Hillman's store. Automatically she looked in the window. She could see past the display of suits and shirts into the store itself. There were no customers in the store and the two young assistants were busy tidying the stock. There was no sign of Tom Hillman.

She continued up the street another block to the Town Hall. She glanced across the street to see the progress that was being made on the clinic construction site. Next door the real estate office was in darkness. The next thing which caught her eye brought her to a standstill. Even her heart seemed to miss a beat.

Beyond the real estate office was the alley which led to the parking lot. Beyond the alley was the bank. In the front wall of the bank was a night depository used by business people to deposit their day's receipts. A man had just used a key to open this depository and was placing the specially locked satchel in the chute. This man was Tom Hillman.

After the momentary state of paralysis she experienced, Cathy glanced at her watch again. It was exactly five fifteen. Was it Tom Hillman's custom to make his bank deposit at this time every day? The answer to this simple question now assumed some importance.

Chapter 27.

Tom Hillman banged the gavel calling the meeting to order. As Chairman of the committee he first welcomed Cathy Silcox as the newly appointed Council representative. The other Council members on the committee were Jim Stevens in his ex-officio capacity as mayor, and Derek Wheeler. The latter had been a citizen appointee prior to his election to Council. There were several other citizen appointees including Joe Simmons. Cathy was the only female member. Two other men were present in addition to the committee members. Harry McLaughlin served as a non-voting technical advisor in matters of legislation and finance, and Jack Porter was there to report on the proceedings for the Record.

"I think," said Tom Hillman, "we can start working on the wording of our recommendation to Council now. With those figures we approved at the last meeting on the property tax implications, I don't think we'll have any problem getting the proposal through Council."

"That's right," said Jim Stevens, "particularly with the composition of the new Council. It should be plain sailing."

"Of course the hard work's still ahead of us," said Joe Simmons. "We've got to get the land serviced. Water and hydro and sewers all have to be planned as well as the new roads. And then the thing on which it all stands or falls. We have to attract the industries to establish their operations here."

"That's true, Joe," said Tom Hillman. "But you're jumping the gun. We'll have to hire engineers to plan the services and we'll probably have to get a PR firm to launch our campaign to industry. Our first job is to get the project approved by Council."

"That's right," said Derek Wheeler. "We have to get Council's approval before we can go to the Province for funding. The money for the engineering and promotion will come from the new Regional Development Act."

This was all pretty technical, and Cathy realized that she still had a lot to learn.

"Before we start on the wording of the recommendation," said Derek Wheeler, "I'd like to go into the property tax matter a bit more." Cathy pricked up her ears.

"That's not necessary," said Hillman. "We approved the figures at the last meeting."

"I know that," said Wheeler, "But since that meeting I've been studying the figures and I'd like to discuss the matter some more."

"You're out of order," said Hillman and banged the gavel fiercely on the table. "The matter was discussed fully and voted on once. It would take a two thirds majority vote to allow the subject to be re-opened."

Wheeler looked a little taken aback. He had never seen Hillman in the role of the strict parliamentarian before. "Alright," he said. "If you want to do it that way. I didn't intend to create an argument. But I move that the matter of the property tax implications be re-opened for discussion." The motion was seconded by Joe Simmons.

"Now remember," said the chairman, "it needs a two thirds majority to pass this motion."

"Why do you want to open it up again, Derek?" asked Jim Stevens. "Aren't you satisfied that we got the right information last time?"

Derek began to answer the mayor's question, but the gavel was banged down again, interrupting him in mid-sentence.

"This motion is asking for the question to be re-opened for discussion," said Hillman. "You can't start discussing the matter until we take this vote. Now let's take the vote and get on with the meeting. If we keep re-hashing old business we'll never get this project off the ground. All those in favour of the motion to re-open the discussion on taxes, signify by raising the right hand."

Cathy thought fast. There was some undercurrent present that she did not understand. But if Derek's motion passed it would give her an opportunity to learn more of what had taken place at the last meeting. She decided to support the motion.

The chairman counted five raised hands. "Those opposed signify in the same manner," he said. This time three hands were counted. "As chairman, I cast my vote against the motion," he said. "There are five votes in favour of the motion and four against. This does not constitute a two thirds majority. The motion is lost".

The rest of the meeting was devoted to a discussion on the wording of the recommendation. Eventually there was unanimous agreement on this matter, and the meeting was adjourned.

Derek Wheeler came round the table to Cathy. "Some of us usually get together for coffee and a chat after the meetings. Would you like to join us?"

"I'd love to," said Cathy. "Thanks".

Most of the members went home. Only Jim Stevens, Joe Simmons and Jack Porter joined Derek and Cathy at the Hearthside.

"I hope you fellows don't mind if I eat something substantial," said Cathy. "My meal schedule got all messed around today." She ordered a cheeseburger and french fries.

"What got into Tom tonight?" asked Joe. "I've never seen him in a mood like that before."

"He must be pretty mad with you, Derek," said Jim. "He usually comes in for coffee. But he took right off without a word. By the way, what was it that you wanted to discuss about the tax thing?"

"You know Jim, I'm not really sure. I've got a feeling there's something wrong in those figures, or at least in the conclusions we drew from them. I've studied them, and I can't put my finger on what's wrong."

"Then what makes you think there's something wrong?" asked Jim.

"As a matter of fact, it was Cathy here who made me wonder about it at first," said Derek. "She told me that Dick Barrett had been worried ever since the last Commission meeting. I've talked to Susan Barrett and she says the same thing. It seems that he was putting together a report on the tax implications, and after his death the report was stolen. I don't know why. And I don't know what's wrong with those figures. But to me that's enough to take a whole new look at it."

"What Derek says is right," said Cathy. "Ken Davey had the same feeling. And I talked to Debbie Thornton the day before she was killed. She told me that Dick's report was a detailed one on the tax implications."

"Then why was Tom so determined that we shouldn't re-open the matter?" asked Jim.

Nobody had an answer to this question. "When the recommendation comes to Council we can open any part of it to scrutiny, can't we?" asked Derek.

"You're darned right," said Jim. "And I'll make sure we do."

On the way home Cathy, Joe and Derek walked together as far as Derek's house. "You know that night depository you have outside the bank," she said to Derek. "Do people tend to use it at the same time every day?"

He was puzzled by her question. "More or less, I suppose. What makes you ask that?"

"She thinks she's a detective!" interjected Joe. "It's probably something to do with identifying another suspect."

Cathy laughed. "In a way it might be. It might turn out to be quite important. If one of the business people in town were seen making a deposit at a certain time one day, would it be a reasonable assumption that they probably made their deposit at or about that time every day?"

"It might be," Derek said. "But not necessarily. Some people are as regular as clockwork. They close off their cash register at the same time every day, make up their deposit and head off to the bank regardless of anything else. Others don't even make a deposit every day. They use their own safe and maybe only use our depository two or three times a week or when they have a large amount on hand. If you have someone particular in mind I might be able to tell you their normal habit. But you'd have to have a pretty convincing reason for wanting to know."

"I can't tell you that yet," she said. "But I might just take you up on your offer before long."

They had reached Derek's house. They said goodnight to him and walked on together to her apartment.

"Are you coming up for a beer?" Cathy asked.

"Yes, but no more detective talk tonight. Promise?"

She laughed. "I promise!"

They went into the kitchen and she took a beer from the fridge. She opened it and poured it into a glass, and then poured herself a Coke. He put his hands on her waist and turned her gently round to face him.

"Have I told you recently," he asked softly, "that I love you?"

She kissed him lightly. "And I love you too, Joe".

They took their drinks into the other room. Joe sat in his usual chair. Cathy slipped her shoes off, but instead of going to the other chair, she sat on Joe's lap, put an arm around his neck and lay her head down on his shoulder. He put one arm around her waist pulling her closer to him, and ran the fingers of his other hand through her hair.

"Have you thought any more about sharing my house?" he asked.

"Yes, I've thought about it a lot, Joe. But I haven't got an answer for you yet. You really took me by surprise. My job is very important to me. My new responsibilities on Council are important to me. My independence is important to me. You're talking about something that would shake up my whole life, and I'm not sure that I'm ready for that."

"I'm not asking you to give up your job—or your Council seat. I'm not even asking you to give up your name if you don't want to. I'm simply asking you to be my wife to share my life, because I love you."

She turned her face up to him and kissed him again. "I know, Joe. But that means sharing a lot of myself that I've never shared with anyone. It's a serious commitment and it scares me. I like you a lot. I really think I love you. But I'm not sure how much of myself I'm willing to share—even with you. I'm a very selfish person, you know."

It was late when Joe left. By that time Cathy was not so sure about the importance of her independence. Her emotions were pressing her to say `yes, I'll marry you tomorrow'. And yet she held back. Her mind said, `No, not yet. You've got too many other responsibilities'.

She undressed and got into bed. But she didn't go to sleep. She sat up in bed with the light still on as her mind went back over the list of suspects she had drawn up. She felt certain that the two murders were related, and that they were probably the work of the same person. If that were true, then she had to cross both Fred Neilson and Susan Barrett off her list. She had thought at one time of adding the name of Derek Wheeler, but she could find no evidence to justify doing so.

This left Ken Davey as the only one of her original suspects. She certainly had discovered nothing to suggest removing him from the list. However, the events of today certainly left her no choice but to add the name of Tom Hillman, and to put him on an equal with Ken in terms of opportunity and possibly of motive, although she was still confused about this.

She put out the light, pulled the covers up. She mouthed a kiss. "Good night, Joe!" she whispered in the emptiness. "Mmm, I'm even more confused about him!"

Chapter 28.

"If only we could find out how he got Neilson's gun, I think we would have a case," said Inspector Perkins. The two Provincial policemen were again in conference with Carl Montmore in his office.

"Yes," said Bill Gordon. "Everything else seems to fit. Davey admits to being in the office at the crucial time. Barrett was alive a few minutes earlier if we believe Neilson. Davey says that Barrett was already dead when he entered the office, but he can't prove that. He was also in the right place at the right time to have killed the Thornton girl."

"But all you can really say," said Montmore, "is that he had the best opportunity to commit both murders. You really don't have any evidence to show that he killed either one of them. You don't even have a strong motive. And as you say, you can't trace the gun to him. I don't think you've got a case that will stand up yet. In some ways we had a better case against Neilson. At least we know it's his gun, and if he shot Barrett, then Davey would be telling the truth when he says Barrett was already dead when he got back to the office."

"That's true," said the Inspector. "But we had Neilson in custody at the time of the second killing. There's no doubt that Davey was on the spot at the time of both murders. Doesn't that strike you as being too much of a coincidence?"

"I agree with you there," said the local chief. "In fact, I'm quite certain in my own mind that Davey is the man we want. All I'm saying is that we don't have the evidence to prove our case."

"I think we're all agreed," said Bill Gordon, "that Davey probably killed them both. It would also have been easy for him to have faked that burglary when the file was stolen. That would support the red herring which he created when he persuaded Miss Silcox that Barrett's murder had something to do with the industrial park committee. The theft of the file would substantiate that idea."

"What about the anonymous letter to Cathy?" asked Montmore.

"There again, it sounds like Davey," said the sergeant. "She admitted to me that she thought she had used that phrase about curiosity killing the cat when she talked to Davey. And we know how angry he was with her for prying into his movements. You see, it all ties in."

"But it's all circumstantial," said the chief. "It's a long string of probabilities. They all seem to fit together, I can see that. But there still isn't one solid piece of evidence. And we really don't have much of a motive either."

"Oh I don't know," said the Inspector. "I think we've got a good enough motive. Jealousy can be a remarkably strong emotion. It can make men do things that they normally would never consider. We have some witnesses from that real estate banquet who will say that Davey's relationship with the girl was far from platonic. The description of the way they danced, and even more of the way they sat out some of the dances. One woman said his hands were all over her. We've only got his word that there was no emotional attachment between them. And then we know that Barrett had been keeping her pretty late at the office several nights a week. On one occasion at least we know that he drove her home around midnight. That may have been for business reasons. But it's hard to expect the girl's lover, or her ardent admirer or whatever phrase you want to use, to see it that way. I can see Davey getting pretty darned jealous of his partner. I can see him having it out with Barrett that night in the office. I've known murders committed for less compelling reasons than that."

"Alright," said Montmore. "You're beginning to make a case. But that kind of murder is likely to be committed on the spur of the moment. And if somehow Davey had managed to get hold of Neilson's gun, then the killing had to be pre-meditated."

"I don't necessarily buy that `spur-of-the-moment' stuff," said Perkins. "If jealousy was really eating at him, he could have sat there in the next office and worked himself up into such a state that he planned the whole thing step by step in his mind, even to the alibi of the meal up at the restaurant on the highway. A really jealous man could get almost as much pleasure out of planning something like that as he would out of pulling the trigger."

"I guess I wouldn't make much of a defense counsel," said the chief with a laugh. "You're knocking down my arguments pretty nicely. But how about this one? If his relationship with Debbie Thornton was so warm and passionate at the real estate banquet, why did he strangle her to death two hours later?"

"It's quite possible that at the banquet she didn't know he had killed Barrett. She could have discovered that on the way home. He might have told her to prove to her how much he loved her. Or more likely, it might have slipped out unintentionally, or perhaps she read between the lines in something he said. At any rate, my guess is that she told him she couldn't go along with that sort of thing. She didn't want it on her conscience. Either she said she would report it to the police, or that she would walk right out of his life."

"You make it sound almost believable," said the chief.

"But I still want some hard evidence," said Perkins. "We've got to prove how he got the gun. Or we've got to find that file and trace it back to him. Or we've got to prove that he wrote the note to the Silcox woman. Any of those, and preferably all of them, will tie all our probabilities into one big certainty. So get to work, Bill, and let's see if we can wrap the case up this week. I'm not going to arrest him until we get the evidence we need. But we'll keep our eye on him. He may give himself away yet."

"My conversation with Mrs. Neilson this morning proved how easily anyone could have got that gun," said the sergeant.

"Yes, but you also said that Mrs Neilson told you that Davey never visited them."

"That's true. And yet, as I left I saw Davey drive up to the house. I'm not too happy about his story that he wanted to straighten things out with Neilson concerning the timing of their respective visits to Barrett's office. Unless it was to be sure that he didn't tell us something that would land him in trouble."

"You don't think that Davey and Neilson could be in it together, do you?"

"I very much doubt it. But I suppose we can't rule it out."

Chapter 29.

On Tuesday Cathy decided that she must devote the full day to her job. There were too many things that were not getting done. She was able to live up to this resolve until the middle of the afternoon. She was mid-way through the weekly pre-school story hour with a group of youngsters squatting on the big rug in the children's section, when she noticed Jack Porter come in. He went over to the desk to talk to Sally and Cathy continued the story.

Almost half an hour later as the mothers picked up their children, Cathy realized that Jack was still in the library. He was sitting at one of the tables reading the editorial section of the Globe & Mail.

"Hello Cathy!" he said. "Can I have a few minutes of your time?"

"Hello Jack! Yes, come into the office," she said. She deserved a bit of a break anyway, she told herself. "What's on your mind?" she asked.

"I've got some ideas for a feature story," he said. "To let the rest of the world know that Eversleigh is keeping up with the times. You know the kind of thing. 'We don't just talk about feminism here, we practise it'. We've got Cathy Silcox, Librarian: Cathy Silcox, Councillor: Cathy Silcox on the industrial committee: Cathy Silcox, Detective!"

"Oh no," she laughed. "You can forget that bright idea."

"Now just a minute, Cathy," he said. "You've got to remember that you are now a politician. Have you ever heard of a politician who doesn't jump at the chance to get his name—I mean her name—oh hell! I don't know how you say it," he grinned. "You can straighten me out in the article. But you know darned well that any politician would jump at the chance of such a feature story. And you can't tell me that every good champion of the cause of feminism hides her light under a bushel. You all want and need a medium to spread your cause. I'm just offering you the chance to win friends and influence people."

"Thanks Jack! But you've got it all wrong. The kind of story that you are talking about would make me look like a special kind of being, different from the norm. My whole contention about feminism is that ordinary women in ordinary everyday situations should be treated just like people. That any job open to people should be open to all people, male and female. This applies to elected office of course. But it should also apply everywhere else too. I don't want to push the idea that I was elected because I'm a woman, but because I'm a person who has some ideas and some abilities. I don't want to be built up as a freak. I want my experience to be the norm for all women."

"That's great, Cathy. And all I'm doing is giving you the chance to tell other people the same thing you're sitting there telling me."

"Yes, but don't you see, if I were a man you wouldn't come rushing in here to do an article about me. Are you planning to do an article about each of the male Councillors?"

"No, I hadn't intended to," he admitted.

"So," she said, "you've proved my point. But I'll make you an offer. If you agree to do a series of articles on each of the newly elected Councillors without singling me out for any special attention, then I'll go along with your idea."

He thought for a while. "That might not be a bad idea. Let me give it some more thought."

"Fine," she said. "Let me know what you decide."

He was about to leave when something else occurred to him.

"There's something else different about you," he said, "that's worth an article. And it has nothing to do with your being a woman. You've been engaged in some amateur detective activities, trying to find out who murdered Dick Barrett and Debbie Thornton. What about a feature on that?"

"No way, Jack! What kind of fool do you think I am? Do you want me to put in writing the statement that I've been snooping into other people's affairs, or would you like me to give you a list of my suspects so that next week you can print an account of the charges laid against me for slander and libel?"

"You're not being very co-operative," he complained.

"I'm sorry," she said. "But when you're prepared to ask me about some routine mundane matter, I'll give you the benefit of my wisdom."

"Alright. I'll do just that. I'm writing a factual routine news report on last night's meeting of the industrial committee. Why did you vote to have the tax matter re-opened?"

"Because as a new member it would give me a better feel about what we were doing if I could hear more discussion of the details."

"Then can you explain," he asked, "why in the Hearthside after the meeting, both you and Derek Wheeler suggested there was something wrong with the figures, and that Dick Barrett's death might have something to do with the fact that he had discovered what was wrong?"

"Now," she said, "let me ask you, are you still writing a factual routine news story on the committee meeting, or a feature article on `Gossip at the Hearthside'?"

"Cathy, you're impossible! Now, look. I'm going to put away my reporter's notebook and pencil for a minute." He matched his words with action. "Now let me tell you something. I don't know how much you know about these murders. I don't know how much you suspect. But I gather that you think there is some connection between the tax implications of the industrial park and the death of Dick Barrett. At the time of Dick's death I was tempted myself to do some detective work. But I gave up on that idea. However, it's just possible that I can help you. After listening to you and Derek in the restaurant last night, I did some thinking. This morning I did some checking, and there is something wrong with those figures, Cathy. I can't explain it now. But if you come down to my office when you have an hour or two to spare, I think I can show you something that might be the thing that Dick Barrett spotted."

"Are you serious, Jack?"

"Absolutely serious. But it's not something you can rush through, so don't come tomorrow. The paper goes to press on Thursday and Wednesday is a mad house down there. Maybe I've got your curiosity aroused a little, but you're going to have to wait until Thursday at least."

"Jack, you're a beast!"

He stood up. "I must go now," he said, "and put the finishing touches to some of my stories. It's a good thing that some people have been more co-operative than you or there wouldn't be any paper this week."

She looked at her watch. It was already after five o'clock.

"I'll walk with you as far as the post office," she said. ""I have to get some stamps."

She took her time in the post office. As she came out she glanced across the street. Tom Hillman was walking past the real estate office with a night deposit satchel in his hand. Cathy looked at her watch. It was thirteen minutes past five.

Chapter 30.

"Sergeant Gordon? This is Cathy Silcox. I have some information that might be important to you. Can you drop over to the library some time this morning?"

When he had agreed to her request, the detective hung up the receiver and turned to the Inspector. "I honestly don't know what to think about that woman!" he said.

"The librarian again?" asked Perkins.

"Yes. She says she has more information. She tries to give me the impression that she's being totally frank and honest and open with me. But I always get the idea that she only tells me what she wants me to know. I'm sure she knows more than she is prepared to tell. In fact, I've caught her a couple of times."

"You'd better go and see what she wants," said the Inspector. "You never know, she might just have the one fact that we need to wrap up the case against Davey."

Cathy greeted the sergeant with a smile. "You're getting to be a stranger, almost," she said. "You never come to see me unless I call you."

As on previous occasions, her smile made Bill Gordon feel uncomfortable. It was a warm, pleasant smile, yet he had the feeling that in reality she was laughing at him.

"What evidence have you got for me this morning?" he asked as he sat in the chair by the window.

"There you go again, Sergeant!" Now he knew that smile was a laugh. She was teasing him. "You're mixing up evidence and information again. I told you that I had some information for you. It's up to you to decide whether or not it's evidence." She told him about her conversation with Millie Brownlee; the response of Tom Hillman to the proposal to re-open the tax issue; the discovery of Tom's apparently regular bank deposit at five fifteen, and the location of his house in relation to Debbie Thornton's apartment.

"I sat up late last night, Sergeant, trying to decide whether or not I should tell you all this. Finally the thought that you might be angry with me again helped me to decide."

The twinkle in her eye confirmed that she was, in fact, teasing him and he didn't know how to handle that.

"Alright," he said crossly, "now you've told me. I hope you feel better. But when are you going to listen to my advice? When will you stop poking your nose into this case?"

"Sergeant, that's not nice! You'll make me wish I hadn't called you."

He ignored her comment. He asked her for Miss Brownlee's address, thanked her and left. Before he returned to the police station he visited Millie Brownlee and also checked on some of the other things Cathy had told him.

"Her story hangs together," he told the Inspector. "It's all circumstantial, but it's certainly possible. All of it's possible."

The two officers studied the case against Tom Hillman and compared it with the facts they had learnt about Ken Davey.

"You know what she's done?" said Perkins. "She's thrown a big monkey wrench into the case!"

"Yes, I think you're right."

"No matter how you look at it," continued Perkins, "we now have two equally strong cases against two different men, each of them built on circumstantial evidence. In each case we have a person with the opportunity to commit both murders. But in neither case can we show how they got access to the gun."

"Just a minute." interrupted Gordon. "I told you that I had discovered one easy way for the gun to have been stolen. Mrs. Neilson told me that Davey had never been to their house. I didn't ask her about Hillman. That needs checking out."

"Yes, it's a point," agreed the Inspector. "But it's unlikely. Weren't Neilson and Hillman opposing candidates for the Reeve's chair?"

"That's true."

"Then they probably weren't on visiting terms."

"Maybe so," said the sergeant, "But not necessarily. And there's another point. If Hillman is the murderer and he wanted someone to frame to take the rap, what better choice than his political opponent?"

"That sounds more like American politics than Canadian!" laughed the Inspector.

"Don't laugh," said Gordon. "A man who will kill won't have any conscience about keeping his politics clean."

"You may be right, Bill. You'd better see what you can find out. The thing that bothers me is that we almost had a case sewn up on Davey. Now we've got as much evidence against Hillman. We can't make another move without one more piece of the jig saw. There is one thing you should do, though. Find out what Hillman and Barrett were arguing about the day before the murder. That may be important in terms of motive. What was it Hillman said to him?"

The sergeant checked his notes. "I'm not going to let you do it. I'll find a way to stop you," he read. "Yes, I must find out what he meant by that. And I'll have another talk with Mrs. Neilson and see if Hillman was at their house in recent weeks."

After several attempts with the bell push and the big brass knocker the sergeant decided that no one was home at the Neilson house. As he strode back down the path to his car the door of the house next door opened.

"They've gone away," called Nellie McLaughlin.

"Gone away?" echoed Bill Gordon in disbelief. He knew that the Inspector had asked Fred Neilson not to leave town, even to go to work.

"Yes," said Nellie. "They've gone to Jill's mother's to get the children back. They left first thing this morning. It's a long drive, so they plan to stay overnight and come home tomorrow."

"Are you sure about that?"

"Oh yes!" Nellie had now come out and joined him on the sidewalk. "Jill told me last night. She took the children to her mother's last week after you people arrested Fred. They were having a hard time at school with the other kids talking about their father. But they talked it over yesterday and decided they couldn't let the children miss any more school. Now that you've let Fred go, they thought the talk might die down."

"I see," said the detective. He made a mental note to report the fact to the Inspector as soon as possible.

"Are you fairly friendly with the Neilson's?" he asked.

"Oh yes," she replied. "We see a lot of each other."

"Do you happen to know whether they were on good terms with the Hillman's?"

"It's funny you should ask that," she said. "Until a couple of months ago they were quite friendly. They even visited back and forth in each other's homes. They used to discuss politics a lot. I remember one evening I was over there when they had the Hillman's in for the evening. Tom and Fred spent the whole evening arguing about the industrial park. I remember thinking that it was strange for such good friends to have such opposite views."

"Was their argument kept on a friendly level?" he asked. He tried not to show how important he considered the information she had just given him.

"Yes. They just disagreed. They never got nasty with one another. Tom wanted the town to grow. He said to do that we had to have new industry. Fred said he came to live here because he wanted to get away from industry. Tom had been in town politics for years. He knew what he was talking about. Then Fred decided to challenge him for the Reeve's chair. He made a big issue out of this industrial park."

"Did this break up their friendship?" asked the detective.

"I don't think so. Of course, they didn't spend much time together after that. They were both too busy with their campaigns for social visiting. But even though they were opponents in politics I don't think they became enemies or anything like that."

"Thank you, Mrs. McLaughlin. You've been a great help."

"I have?" She looked puzzled as she went back into the house. She made herself a cup of coffee and sat down to think of some reason the detective might have found their conversation helpful to him. She was unable to reach any conclusion. She hoped that she hadn't said anything she shouldn't.

When he arrived back at the station Bill Gordon reported on the out-of-town trip taken by the Neilson's. He was more than a little deflated by the Inspector's response.

"Yes, I know. Didn't I tell you? Neilson called last night to ask my permission to go and get his kids back. He told me where he was going and promised to be back tomorrow."

Bill Gordon looked cheated. "But you knew I was going round there. Why didn't you tell me?"

"Don't get sore, Bill! He only asked for permission for himself to go. Of course, he didn't need permission for his wife to leave town, but I assumed he was going on his own. And you said you were going to talk to Mrs. Neilson. But there's no harm done."

"No," said Gordon. "In fact there was quite a bit of good done". He related his conversation with Nellie McLaughlin. "So you see, Hillman had lots of opportunity to get his hands on that gun."

"You're right. That fills a gap. We have to consider him now as much of a prime suspect as Davey. Of course, we still haven't proved that he actually took the gun. And I'd still like to know more about that argument he had with Barrett."

Chapter 31.

Shortly after Sergeant Gordon left the library that morning Gail Redshaw came in and asked for Cathy.

"Hi, Cathy, how you doing? I've brought you some homework."

She held out a large manilla envelope addressed to Cathy.

"Homework?"

"Yes. It's your agenda for tonight's Council meeting, and all the stuff you're supposed to read before the meeting. You don't have anything else to do, do you? I'm sorry. I usually try to get it out a couple of days before the meeting, but things have been so hectic."

"That's O.K., Gail. Thanks anyway. I guess I'll just have to make time to read the stuff."

The large envelope contained the detailed agenda for the Council meeting. Behind the agenda were several pages of reports and recommendations from various committees. These reports related to items on the agenda and provided resource material to assist the Councillors in making their decisions. Stapled to the top left hand corner of the agenda was a smaller sheet of paper. This sheet contained a brief apology from Harry for the lateness of the agenda. No reason was given for the delay, simply the apology.

Cathy glanced through the agenda. Most of the items appeared to be fairly routine. The only one likely to generate any great excitement was the recommendation of the industrial Park committee. She flipped the pages until she came to the text of this report. She took it to her desk. She sat down, lit a cigarette and read through the report and recommendations with considerable concentration. As an appendix to the report she found the detailed figures on the property tax implications of the proposal. As she stared at these figures she stubbed out the end of her cigarette and, without thinking, lit another one. She examined the figures from every point of view she could think of, challenging them to give up the secret she believed them to be hiding.

Finally she had to admit that she could see nothing wrong with the figures. She found the whole presentation to be clear and convincing. If it were not for the link that she still believed existed between the report and the two murders, she knew she would give it her wholehearted support at the Council meeting. But what was the hidden secret? She had to know!

She put the papers back into their original order and placed them on a corner of the desk. She got up and walked over to the window where she stood deep in thought. It was snowing and the wind was blowing the snow into drifts across the lawn. As the white flakes swirled aimlessly in the air, so a jumble of thoughts swirled through her mind. It didn't seem possible that it was only two weeks ago today that Dick Barret had been murdered. So much had happened in her life in those two weeks. She had learnt so much in that time. But there was still too much she didn't know. Would they ever find out for sure who the murderer was? Would they ever know how the murders were related to the plans for the industrial park. That they were somehow related she still believed. But how? And Who?

The telephone on her desk rang. It was Joe Simmons. He wanted her to know that he intended to come to the Council meeting tonight. He would be sitting in the visitors area. He was anxious to hear how Council dealt with the committee's recommendations, and he wanted to see if any new information came to light relative to the tax figures. While she was listening to him her eyes strayed to the pile of papers on her desk. Suddenly something about those papers attracted her attention. When she finished her conversation with Joe she replaced the receiver and examined the papers again.

With a throb of excitement she grabbed her coat and rushed out of her office. She told Sally that she had to go down to see Jack Porter at the Record office on a matter of extreme importance. She said she would be back in time to relieve her at the desk at lunch time. It was snowing harder now and Cathy pulled the large collar of her coat up around her ears. The snow hadn't been forecast in the morning and she hadn't worn her boots. She slipped several times as she rushed down the street. She burst into Jack Porter's office without knocking. "Jack, I've got to talk to you," she said breathlessly.

He looked up from his desk with a frown. "Cathy, please, not today! I told you that Wednesday is the day we go to press. I still have several articles to finish. I just can't take the time to talk to you today. Come back tomorrow."

She didn't appear to have noticed the desperation in his voice.

"Jack, this is really important! You've got to help me. You've got to tell me what you know about those tax figures."

"I will, Cathy. I promise you. I'll explain it all to you tomorrow. But today you must leave me alone."

"No, Jack! I have to know today. I have to know before tonight's Council meeting."

He began to get angry. "Now listen, Cathy. I'm not fooling. This paper has to go on the press tonight. I don't have any choice about that. Can't you understand? Either you get out right now and leave me alone until tomorrow, or I will physically pick you up and throw you through that door."

He stood up and prepared to put his threat into effect.

Cathy reacted with a flash of anger to match his.

"I'm warning you, Jack Porter." she said, "that if you throw me out without the information I want, I shall go straight to the police station. And I will return very quickly with those two O.P.P. officers. When I tell my story to them they won't give you a minute's peace until you tell them the facts about those tax figures."

She saw the slight look of hesitation on his face. He opened his mouth to say something, but before he could get a word out she continued, "If you don't believe I mean that, then go ahead and call my bluff. But I'm warning you, you'll regret it. I know from personal experience that if Sergeant Gordon thinks you're not telling him everything you know he'll give you no peace. He's like a terrier with a slipper. He won't let go until he satisfies himself you've given him every detail. So which way do you want it? Do you want to tell me or Sergeant Gordon?"

Porter was definitely wavering. He sat down again behind his desk.

"What's got into you Cathy? I've never seen you like this."

She realized that she had got his attention. She knew now that he would co-operate. Before answering his question she sat down across the desk from him. She lit a cigarette and blew out a cloud of smoke. Her voice was calmer and more controlled.

"What's got into me, Jack, is that I'm sure I have just discovered who the murderer is. If you will tell me what you know about that tax table, I have a feeling that it will provide me with confirmation of what I have discovered and will also give me a way of exposing the murderer."

She paused, keeping her eyes on him as she inhaled deeply and blew another cloud of smoke.

"And you and your newspaper will have the biggest scoop of your career".

She sat back and crossed her legs. She smiled at the startled look of disbelief on his face.

"Do you know what you are saying?" he asked.

"I certainly do!" Her voice now carried a new note of confidence.

"Then who is the murderer?" he asked.

"I can't tell you now," she said. "But I am confident that the information you give me about those taxes will make it possible for me to reveal the murderer's identity to you later today."

"Will you tell me before the news hounds in the city get it?"

She answered with another question. "Will you be at the Council meeting tonight?"

"Yes".

"Then you'll get the news before the rest of the media. Now what about those figures?"

"Come into the back room," he said, leading the way. It took him the best part of an hour to show her what he had discovered. As she had anticipated, the information confirmed her conviction about the identity of the murderer.

"Thanks, Jack! Now get back to your paper. I'll see you at Council tonight. And I suggest that you leave some space on your front page for a big story. You may be up all night writing it!"

As she left the office she hesitated on the sidewalk. Should she go straight to Bill Gordon with the information that she had, or should she try to play a lone hand? She glanced at her watch. She really must get back to the library and let Sally go to lunch.

She was kept busy at the desk without a free moment throughout Sally's lunch break. As soon as Sally returned, Cathy left the library. She went to the Hearthside and was able to find a small table that was empty in the rear of the restaurant. Here, over home made soup and a Caesar salad she could think and plan the steps she had to take later in the day.

She was now certain that she knew the identity of the murderer as well as the motive that led to Dick Barrett's death. She made an educated guess at the motive for the other murder. There were, however, still a few vital facts that she needed to know. She had no doubt that she could prove that the opportunity was there in the case of the first murder, although she was not quite so sure in the case of Debbie's death. And she still didn't know how the murderer had gained access to the gun. Despite these gaps in her knowledge she was sure she had enough facts to expose the criminal's identity. Obviously she must share this information with the police. But exactly how and when should she do this? She didn't want the police to jeopardize the plan she had worked out.

She returned to the library without resolving this question. As she entered the front door she noticed Nellie McLaughlin checking out her weekly selection of light novels. She realized that if Nellie saw her, she would have to listen to the usual fifteen or twenty minutes of town gossip, and she could do without that today. She tried to slip into her office unnoticed. She was unsuccessful.

"Why, hello Cathy!" How are you?"

"I'm fine, Mrs. McLaughlin. How's everything with you?" asked Cathy in an easy and pleasant manner which did not indicate the impatience and frustration she felt.

"Oh just the same as usual, dear. How are you enjoying Council?" Nellie asked, but didn't pause long enough for a reply. "Harry tells me you're going to be a great asset on Council. He says you're very conscientious and do your homework well."

"There hasn't been much opportunity for me to prove that yet," said Cathy. "But I'll do my best. Where's your neighbour today?"

It was most unusual for Nellie to visit the library without having Jill Neilson in tow.

"Oh, Fred and Jill have gone down to her mother's to bring the children home," she said. "It's a long drive so they're staying overnight. They'll be back tomorrow. And that reminds me," she went on.

It seemed that everything that Nellie McLaughlin said reminded her of something else she wanted to say.

"That reminds me, I have to buy some cat food. Jill asked me to look after their cat again. She said they used the last can of cat food last night. I hope it doesn't go on another hunting spree tonight."

Cathy looked a little puzzled. The reference to the `hunting spree' was meaningless to her. She knew Nellie well enough not to ask for an explanation.

Nellie, however, didn't need asking. She caught that look of puzzlement, slight as it was.

"Last time we looked after the cat, the night Jill took the children to her mother's, the cat went off on the tiles, and it took Harry ages to find it. He went over in the evening to let it out for a walk and check that it had enough food and water. But the damned cat didn't come back. And they're very fussy about it being in the house at night. Harry was gone for ages looking for it."

After several more items of neighbourhood information had been dispensed, Nellie allowed Sally to check her books out. She left the library, presumably in search of cat food.

Cathy could not concentrate on her work. She felt guilty at the amount of time she had taken off in the past two weeks. When this mess was all cleared up she'd try and do something special for Sally to thank her for the way she had pitched in without a grumble. The feeling of guilt, however, was not strong enough to keep her at the library for the rest of the afternoon. She simply had to get away and make some decisions. She quieted her conscience with the assurance that her moonlighting days as a detective were almost over.

"Sally, if you don't mind, I have to leave early again. Will you lock up? I'll see you in the morning".

She gathered up the pile of papers, slipped them back into the big envelope, and went home. She kicked off her shoes, got a bottle of Coke out of the refrigerator, and went to her favourite chair. With her feet tucked beneath her and a cigarette lit, she settled into her most productive thinking position.

Despite the two bits of information which still caused a frustrating gap in her knowledge, she formulated a carefully planned procedure which she felt sure would expose the truth. The one question left to be decided was whether she should inform the police before or after she set her plan into motion. The thought of the possible danger she might be putting others in as well as herself, finally tipped the balance. She picked up the telephone and called Sergeant Bill Gordon.

Chapter 32.

"No, Sergeant. I'm not fooling. I'm not throwing red herrings. I've never in my life been more serious. I have some real solid evidence. In fact, I believe that I have enough evidence to constitute proof. I know who the murderer is."

"Are you still at the library?"

"No, I'm at home. I'm just going to get myself a bite to eat. In two hours I have to be at the Council meeting. So you either come up here and listen to what I've got to say, and agree to support me, or I'm going to expose the murderer on my own."

"Stay there. Don't talk to anyone else. I'll be over right away!" said the sergeant with a sigh.

"Can I prepare you a snack while I'm getting myself something?"

"No thanks. I'll eat later." He hung up.

Cathy was still eating when the door bell rang. She let the sergeant in.

"Come in! I hope you don't mind sitting in the kitchen while I finish eating. Are you sure I can't get you something?"

"Quite sure. Thanks all the same. Now what's this all about?"

"I've got coffee on. I'm just going to pour myself a cup. Can I pour you some?"

"Yes, I'll have a coffee. Now look here, Miss Silcox. This is getting very serious. You simply must listen to me. You know what happened to Miss Thornton and you've already had a warning in that anonymous note. If you don't stop poking your nose into things you don't understand, there's going to be a third murder to solve. And you won't be around to solve it."

"Calm down, Sergeant! Don't you remember me telling you that I am by nature a very curious person. There are times when I have an insatiable urge to satisfy my curiosity. This has been one of those times."

"I repeat, Miss Silcox, ` Curiosity killed the cat'."

"Oh stop repeating that stupid saying," she said impatiently. "If you want to use quotations why don't you read some good literature. Then you would realize that there's another value to curiosity."

"What are you talking about?"

"It was Samuel Johnson who wrote—` Curiosity is one of the most permanent and certain characteristics of a vigorous intellect'. And that quotation does more for me than the one about the cat. Here's your coffee. Why don't we take it through to the living room where it's more comfortable?"

Cathy told him in detail the discoveries she had made, including the information she had gained from Jack Porter about the tax figures. She also outlined the plan which she had formulated to expose the truth, as well as the support that she wanted from the police.

The sergeant was appalled by her plan.

"Miss Silcox, you can't do that! Don't you realize the danger?"

"There won't be any danger as long as you do your part, Sergeant."

"Now, listen to me! From everything you have told me, I think you are probably correct in your identification of the murderer. You've certainly uncovered some very strong evidence that points in that direction. And you did the right thing to turn this information over to me without delay. But now you have to be sensible and allow us to follow the normal investigative procedures leading to an arrest. Any other course of action would be suicidal, perhaps literally suicidal!"

But Cathy had made up her mind.

"You can talk all you like about normal procedures," she said. "But in fact you have four choices. And you have a little over an hour to make your choice."

"What do you mean?"

"Choice number one: you can go along with my proposal and provide me with the support I have asked for. Choice number two: you can leave me to go it alone and elect not to provide that support. Choice number three: you can, if you're fast, jump the gun on me and arrest the suspect before I make my presentation. If you make that choice I think you will miss out on the conclusive evidence I think I will generate. Your only other choice, as far as I can see, is to find some grounds to arrest me within the next hour!"

As she lit a cigarette, the smile she bestowed on the sergeant added to his mounting irritation.

"But can't you see that your proposal is completely contrary to accepted police procedures? Even if I were mad enough to go along with your idea, Inspector Perkins would veto it."

"Then you have an hour to change the Inspector's mind for him," she said as she pulled her feet from under her and slipped them into her shoes. She stood up.

"I want to have a shower and change into something decent before the meeting," she said. "I don't mean to be inhospitable, but you may need that time to discuss the matter with your Inspector."

He got up with a grunt. Without another word he strode through the door she held open. Before going to the bathroom she called Joe Simmons.

"Joe, Could you stop over to my place before the Council meeting. Something important has happened and I wanted you to know about it."

"I'll be right over," he replied.

"Don't rush. I'm just going to take a shower and get into something decent. Come over in about half an hour."

She peeled off her clothes and luxuriated in the hot shower as long as she dared. As she dressed she felt a tight knot of nervousness in the pit of her stomach. She had put on her panties and bra and a new pair of panty hose, and was pulling on a nylon slip when the door bell rang. She looked at her watch. It was barely twenty minutes since she had called Joe.

She went to the door and called down—"Who is it?"

She heard steps coming up the stairs. "It's me, Cathy". she recognized Joe's voice. "Hey, I like that!" Joe grinned as he came through the door. "That's what I call being dressed for the occasion!"

He took her into his arms and kissed her. As she relaxed against his body his hands caressed her bare shoulders and slid down to her waist. He pulled her tight against him and kissed her again.

Cathy reluctantly pulled away from him.

"I'm sorry, Joe. It's not that kind of occasion! In half an hour I have to be at Council. Before that I have something to tell you. I can't go to Council dressed like this! Come into the bedroom while I finish dressing and put some make up on."

She led the way. "Sit on the bed if you like," she said over her shoulder as she went to the closet and selected an eyecatching red and white dress which she had bought on a shopping spree to celebrate her election. She pulled it over her head and went over to the bed.

"Zip me up, dear," she said.

"With pleasure," Joe responded with a smile. "This is the kind of little chore I could do for you every day when we're married. Not to say the job of unzipping your dress at the end of the day!"

She laughed as she turned and gave him a quick kiss.

"You don't miss a trick, do you? But be serious for a minute and listen to what I've got to say".

She sat on the stool in front of the mirror and put on a pair of silver earrings and a matching necklace. As she worked on her hair and make up she said, "I know who the murderer is and I'm going to expose him at the Council meeting tonight."

Joe leapt to his feet. "What on earth are you talking about?" he exclaimed.

"Sit down and listen, Joe. I don't have much time." She repeated the facts that she had outlined earlier to Bill Gordon, including the plan she had devised to expose the murderer.

He was horrified. "You can't do that, Cathy!" he yelled. "It's dangerous. He'll attack you! You've got to turn it over to the police now. Let them finish the job".

"I talked to Sergeant Gordon just before I called you. I told him the facts. I told him what I'm going to do. I asked him to have the police ready to intervene at the right moment."

"Surely he didn't agree to your mad scheme?" asked Joe, his face expressing disbelief.

"I admit he took some convincing. Now he's gone off to talk to his Inspector. I don't think I gave him much choice."

Cathy went back to the closet to get a pair of black high heel pumps which she put on. She turned to face him.

"There." she said, "How do I look?"

"You look even more stunning than usual! But you're mad!"

"Come on, Joe. There's no more time for talk. We've got to go."

He helped her on with her coat and as they went out she picked up a bulging brief case.

Chapter 33.

The ground floor of the Town Hall consisted of a meeting room on one side and the Council Chamber on the other side of a wide hallway. Across the back of the building, opening off a narrower hallway which formed a T with the other, were a number of small offices. These included the offices of Carl Montmore and Harry McLaughlin. The doors of these two offices faced the wide hallway, while other offices, including the rest of the police department and secretaries, were located to either side of them.

As Joe and Cathy entered the Town Hall they walked down the hallway to the offices instead of going directly into the Council Chamber. The door of the police chief's office was ajar. Cathy knocked on it, and without waiting for a reply stuck her head round the door.

"Hello!" she said "I'm glad to see you're all here. Are you ready for action?"

Carl Montmore sat behind his desk. He was the only one who appeared to be at ease.

"Miss Silcox, I'd like to talk to you," said the big Inspector as he got up from his chair.

Cathy smiled. "It will have to be after the Council meeting, I'm afraid. They must be ready to start the meeting."

Before he could say another word she was on her way back down the hallway. He reached the office door, almost tripping over Bill Gordon's feet, just in time to see her enter the Council Chamber.

"Damn that girl!" he exclaimed.

Joe grasped the Inspector's arm. "Do you know what she's planning to do? Isn't she putting herself in a dangerous situation?"

"Of course she is! But she's as stubborn as a mule." He paused and looked at Joe. "What do you know about it?" he asked.

"She called me just after she had talked to your sergeant. She told me what she was going to do. I tried to talk her out of it. But, as you say, she's stubborn. I don't like what's happening, though."

"Neither do we," said the Inspector. "But all we can do now is to be ready at the door to jump in at the right moment. Are you going into the meeting?"

"Yes. I'm going to the visitor's section now. I'll keep my eye on things, but I don't mind telling you that I'm nervous."

* * * * * * * * * *

Jim Stevens banged the gavel to bring the meeting to order. The minutes of the last meeting were approved and a number of routine matters were dealt with.

"The next item on the agenda is the report and the recommendations from the industrial committee," said the mayor. "Tom, you're chairman of the Commission. Will you present the report."

Tom Hillman went through the report fairly rapidly as all the members had received copies.

"Now we come to the recommendations," he said. "And, of course, the main one is that we proceed with the project as described in the report. All the other recommendations deal with the steps to be taken in implementing the project. The most important thing we want to achieve tonight is to have Council set their seal of approval on the whole project. This is of such vital importance to the future of this town that I don't think there has been a more significant issue to come before us in all the time I have sat on this Council. A positive decision tonight will move us toward an exciting future. I therefore move that recommendation number one be approved as printed."

"There are some questions that I have about certain aspects of the report," said Derek Wheeler, "but for the purposes of discussion, I will second the motion."

"The motion is now before you for discussion," declared the mayor.

"I would like to speak to the motion, your worship," said Cathy Silcox.

Now that the time had come, her throat felt dry and there was a weakness in her knees. She hoped that Bill Gordon had convinced the Inspector to have reinforcements at the ready.

"As the newest member of the committee," she began, "I have not had the benefit of sharing in all the deliberations with the other members. But I have done some homework this past week. As the report makes clear, one of the strongest arguments in favour of this project is the tax benefit that would be gained by every Eversleigh taxpayer. If the figures in the appendix are accurate, then it would be hard for anyone to vote against the recommendation. It would seem, therefore, to be of some considerable importance for us to examine these figures to determine their accuracy."

"We don't need to do that at this point," interrupted Tom Hillman. "The accuracy of the figures has already been established."

"Do I have the floor, your worship?" asked Cathy.

"You do, Councillor Silcox. I would ask all members to refrain from interrupting."

Tom Hillman's face and neck were red with anger.

"I am not alone in questioning these figures," continued Cathy. "One of the original members of the committee, Dick Barrett, spent many hours checking this matter. It is my understanding that he had completed his work and was ready to report his findings at the time of his death. His secretary, Miss Debbie Thornton, had worked on this matter with him, and less than a week later she also met with a sudden death. Shortly after that a file containing Dick's report was stolen from his office. Now, as some of you are aware, I have been making enquiries into the circumstances of these murders."

"Point of order, your worship." The interruption again came from Tom Hillman.

"State your point of order," said the mayor.

"Your worship, the subject under discussion is the report of the industrial park committee, not the investigation of murder."

"Your worship," said Cathy, bestowing on the mayor one of her most charming smiles, "If you will allow me to continue, I promise that almost immediately I will connect my investigation directly to the report we are presently considering."

"You may continue," said the mayor.

"Thank you, your worship. As I think back over the course of my investigations, and particularly the relationship that I believe existed between the murder and the tax figures, I am reminded of a certain quotation. It is a quotation about a cat."

She paused and looked around at her listeners. She noticed the almost imperceptible tightening of the face muscles of one person.

"It was Mark Twain," she went on, "who wrote this—'We should be careful to get out of an experience only the wisdom that is in it—and stop there; lest we be like that cat that sits down on a hot stove lid. She will never sit down on a hot stove lid again—and that is well: but also she will never sit down on a cold one any more'.

"Your worship, I learnt this lesson both in my investigation of the murders and in my study of the tax situation. We are all guilty at times, like the cat, of reading more into an experience than the wisdom that is in it.

"Now I have in my hand a sheet of paper. This paper contains some facts that I was able to verify this morning. I am going to ask, your worship, that you arrange to have this paper turned over to the Provincial Auditor's office for his official verification. When you have agreed to do that, I am going to move that the report of the Industrial Commission be tabled until we receive official word from the Provincial Auditor. I believe this will show that there are some gross inaccuracies in these tax figures."

There were several audible gasps, followed by the buzz of whispered conversation. The mayor banged the gavel again.

"Order!" he demanded.

"May I have two more minutes, your worship?" asked Cathy.

"Continue," said the mayor.

"Thank you. Within those two minutes it is my intention to, if you'll excuse another cat quotation, 'let the cat out of the bag'. This, in fact, is exactly what Dick Barrett was about to do when he was shot to death. I became curious about this mystery, and in conversation with Sergeant Gordon of the Provincial Police, I was warned that 'curiosity killed the cat'".

She smiled at the faces which were now all turned towards her.

"I'm sorry about all these cat quotations, but you see a cat, a real live cat, is a vital part of the solution to this matter. Last week I received a threatening anonymous letter reminding me of the curiosity quotation. It was not until I received the agenda for tonight's meeting that I realized who had sent me that anonymous letter. At that moment I guessed what was wrong with the tax figures. I now know what Dick Barrett knew. Because of what he knew, he was killed. And forgive me for this, but it is true. A cat entered into both of those murders.

"A cat being cared for by a neighbour provided the opportunity to steal the weapon that killed Dick Barrett. The same cat, supposedly on a hunting spree, provided a late night alibi for the second murder."

The silence was shattered by the noise of a chair sliding backwards into the wall with a crash.

"You damned interfering bitch!" yelled Harry McLaughlin as he leapt across the table at Cathy.

Before he reached her his arms were pinned to his side by three policeman who rushed into the room at his first movement. One of them produced a pair of handcuffs which he had round Harry's wrists before the mayor's gavel could be heard above the uproar. Cathy felt faint, but looked over at the visitor's section and smiled weakly at Joe as the policemen led their prisoner from the room.

Chapter 34.

Much later in the evening there was another gathering around a big table at the Hearthside.

"Why did you want me to come over, Cathy?" asked Ken Davey.

"As you had been one of my leading suspects, I thought you had a right to be in at the kill," she said with a grin. "Forgive the inappropriate terminology. And forgive me for all the bad thoughts I've had about you recently! If Fred Neilson hadn't been out of town, I'd have asked him too."

Jack Porter had already gone off to re-write his front page. He would probably be up all night. The others around the table included Jim Stevens, Tom Hillman, Derek Wheeler and Joe Simmons.

"Cathy, I'm sorry that I seemed to be such an obstructionist," said Tom Hillman.

"I'll forgive you, Tom," she said "But you've no idea how close it got you to being convicted for murder!"

"Me?" he asked incredulously.

Cathy laughed. "Yes, you. Once you started objecting to a review of the figures you just about sealed your fate. You know that you were overheard threatening Dick Barrett the day before he was killed?"

For a moment he looked blank. Then a sudden look of comprehension spread across his face.

"Oh, now I remember. I can see how someone might have read that the wrong way. Dick told me that he had discovered something that meant the industrial park would have to be delayed. He wouldn't tell me what it was. He just said he'd fill in all the details at the next meeting. I remember I was pretty peeved at him. That project is important to me. I've put a lot of myself into it and I didn't want someone wrecking the whole thing on a minor technicality. I guess I did get a bit mad with him. Of course, I had no idea what he had discovered."

"Well, that was just about enough to convict you," said Cathy. "Particularly when I discovered that you make a bank deposit at about five fifteen every day right next door to Dick's office. Not only that, but your house backs onto Debbie Thornton's."

"Good heavens!" His smile faded. "You really were getting into this thing with a vengeance, weren't you?"

"Now, Cathy," said Ken, "Tell us what really happened, and how you found out."

"The first real solid clue came this morning when I got the agenda," she said. "Before that I was just like that cat on the hot stove. I was reading all kinds of things into ordinary innocent occurrences. But when I recognized that the note attached to the corner of the agenda came from the same funny-shaped scratch pad as the anonymous letter I had received, then everything fell into place. It was an unusual shape—sort of long and very narrow.

"Then I talked to Jack Porter. He had discovered what Harry had been doing. He had been keeping a double set of books in his office. He was embezzling tax money, but the false set of books balanced with the bank statements. He had been doing this for several years, and had never been caught. But in order to keep this up he had to present false figures on the tax expectations for the budget. You see there were thousands of dollars a year involved. I don't know how much, but it was pretty significant.

"Evidently Dick Barrett had discovered this. He knew the assessed value of all the property in town. It was part of his business. I suspect that he had prepared his own forecast and when Harry's figures were very different he put in a lot of hours with Debbie's help to discover where the discrepancies were. I think he probably faced Harry with the facts, and maybe told him that he was going to report his findings to Council. That would explain why he had to be killed before the first Council meeting.

"The week-end before the murder the Neilson's went away. Harry and Nellie lived next door and they looked after the Neilson cat when they were away. Harry had to let it in and out of the house, and of course they had left him their key. It was no secret that Jill Neilson had a gun, and it was easy for Harry to get it when he let the cat in.

"On the day of the murder he had taken some papers over to the hospital. He would use the alley beside Dick's office. He must have slipped in the side door just after Fred Neilson left. No one would hear the shot because of the construction equipment. Just after he came back across the street, he saw you come out of the front door of the office, Ken. He probably thought that you'd come straight from your own office and hadn't seen Dick. It wasn't until later that he discovered you had told the police you were out of town. That was when he saw the chance to frame you."

"But how did he know what I had told the police?"

"His office is right next to Carl Montmore's. Both offices get pretty stuffy and they often leave their doors open. If you're perfectly quiet in one office, I suspect you can hear every word next door. He probably heard Bill Gordon tell the Inspector about my `curiosity and the cat' proverb too. He may have had an idea that I was on to him, so he sent me that anonymous letter.

"Then somehow he discovered that Debbie Thornton knew about the tax embezzlement. Maybe she told him. At any rate, she now had to be silenced. The night that Jill Neilson took her kids to her mother's Harry had to look after the cat again. My guess is that he got the cat into the Neilson house, then dashed over to Debbie's place. She wasn't home, so he waited for her. That meant that he was away longer than he should have been. When she came back with you, Ken, you dropped her off at the front of the house, didn't you?"

"That's right."

"She had to come around the side of the house to the outside stairs that led up to her apartment. Harry must have been waiting at the bottom of the stairs. He strangled her and when he got home he explained to his wife his long absence by saying that the cat had gone on a hunting spree and he couldn't find it. Nellie dropped that piece of information on me out of the blue at the library. She obviously didn't realize the significance of her words. That's the whole story, except that Harry must have found some way to steal Dick's file before anyone else read it and realized it's importance."

"But how did you figure all that out, Cathy?" asked Jim Stevens.

"Once I spotted the similarity of the scratch pad sheets the rest all fell into place. I should have thought about the cat business before, especially with all the talk about curiosity killing the cat."

They were just about to leave when Bill Gordon came in. He was smiling. Cathy had never seen him smile before. She thought it made him look a lot more human. "Congratulations, Cathy!" he said. "Thanks for your help. You don't mind me calling you Cathy, do you?"

"Not at all, Bill," she laughed. "But you won't forget what Samuel Johnson said about the virtue of curiosity, will you?"

"I'll remember. By the way, who was it that said that there's more than one way to skin a cat?"

Cathy put her arm through Joe's as they walked together to her apartment.

"Can I come up for a while?" he asked. "I know it's very late, but there are a couple of pieces of unfinished business I have to attend to."

"Sure. Come on up."

She looked at her watch. "It's way after midnight. The neighbours are going to start talking about us."

Joe laughed. "They'd talk a lot more if I did my unfinished business out here on the sidewalk!"

When they'd hung up their coats Cathy reached into her purse for her cigarettes. Joe stopped her, took her into his arms and said, "This is even more important than a smoke! The time has come for an answer. You've finished your other big project. Now tell me, will you marry me?"

"Oh, Joe! I do love you!" she sighed as she lay her head on his shoulder and clung to him. He raised her face to his and kissed her with intense passion. He moved his lips up her cheek and kissed her ear gently. Then he whispered, "You haven't given me your answer yet. Will you marry me?"

"Joe, darling! I can think of so many sensible reasons to say no. But my heart won't let me." She pulled her face away from him so that she could look into his eyes. "Yes, Joe! I'll marry you!"

It was several minutes before they completed the next kiss. As their lips finally separated, Cathy said, "There were two pieces of unfinished business you wanted to attend to. What was the other?"

He chuckled mischievously. "Elementary, my dear sleuth! Earlier this evening you gave me the job of zipping up your dress. Surely you also need me to finish the job!" As he spoke, his fingers found the zipper at the back of her neck and began to gently easy it downwards.

Would you like to see your manuscript become a book?

If you are interested in becoming a PublishAmerica author, please submit your manuscript for possible publication to us at:

acquisitions@publishamerica.com

You may also mail in your manuscript to:

**PublishAmerica
PO Box 151
Frederick, MD 21705**

www.publishamerica.com